I0716507

Praise for *MARY ELLEN*

"My sister, Mary Baird Mayer, continues the saga of our family by writing about the life of our remarkable mother, Mary Ellen Sletten Baird, the granddaughter of Isabelle Dahl Anderson Sletten, whose life she wrote about in her first book *Isabelle, Dakota Prairie Pioneer Wife and Mother.* Mary Ellen was nicknamed the "Little Tyke" by her parents, John and Nellie Sletten, our grandparents, because of her small stature. This book is a love story at heart telling of our mother's growing up during the hard years of the depression on the 160-acre South Dakota farm her grandfather, Ingvold Sletten, and her father, John Sletten, purchased in 1917 as the family homestead. It tells of the courtship of her and our father, Clark Baird, whose chance meeting on a college campus led to sixty-six years of marriage. She was born on the family homestead that remains in our family today and in which she and our father raised a family of eight children."

—**Ruth Baird Pollard,** Author of *Loving Gordon: A Dementia Caregiver's Journey*

"Mary Baird Mayer has preserved the cherished stories of her pioneering ancestors by creating a delightful historical journey for her readers. The tale is told through the eyes of one precious foremother born into a loving family challenged with farming a harsh, unpredictable land. As Mary Ellen grows from a "little tyke" into a young woman, she learns what is truly important through enduring the hardships and embracing the joys that come with the rites of passage of a girl in a changing world."

—**Melissa Kale,** Writer, Poet, and Author of *Fabulous Fruit*

Praise for *MARY ELLEN*

"I have had the honor of reading an advance copy of Mary Baird Mayer's new novel, *Mary Ellen.* Not only was it a privilege but a great pleasure. Like in her first novel, *Isabelle,* Mayer has once again displayed her talent in converting an ancestor's private journal into a semi-fiction telling the tale of a woman's life from early childhood. This story is about growing up and coming of age in the darkest times of the twentieth century. The author takes us inside the mind of a young girl with all her joys and fears. We live with her as she grows through grade and then high school. We see Mary Ellen develop and mature into a fledgling college student and finally as a young woman. Travel with Mary Ellen as she learns the realities of life in the 1930s dustbowl of the northern plains. Celebrate with her the victories and try not to shed a tear as we share her pains of loss. I hope you will enjoy this novel as much as I did."

—**Richard Skorupski,** Author of the *Flyover County Series*

MARY ELLEN

Little Tyke Grows Up

MARY BAIRD MAYER

Editing by Melissa Kale • Cover by Rolf Busch • Decorations by Vecteezy.com

Library of Congress Cataloging-in-Publication Data

Mayer, Mary Baird

Mary Ellen: Little Tyke Grows Up

p. cm.

Paperback ISBN: 978-1-947708-80-8 • Ebook ISBN: 978-1-947708-76-1

Library of Congress Control Number: 2022923571

First Edition, December 2022

CITRINE PUBLISHING

State College, Pennsylvania, USA

(828) 585 - 7030

www.CitrinePublishing.com

For my grandmother, Mary Ellen (Nellie) Bixby Sletten,
who risked her life to bring my mother into the world.
She along with my grandfather, John I. Sletten,
raised a strong, loving and very wise woman,
my mother, Mary Ellen.

Mary Ellen at about age three, circa 1920

Mary Ellen at age one, circa 1919

MY EARLY YEARS
1918

I WAS BORN INTO MY Grandma Isabelle's arms on July 20, 1918. She was an experienced midwife and had delivered many babies in her life, including her own nine children, my own papa, John, being one of them. There was a bad rainstorm the night before and the roads were pure mud. Our phone line was out because of the storm so Papa hitched up our horse, old Kit, and rode to the nearest neighbor, only to find their phone was out also. He tried another neighbor and was finally able to call and talk to the doctor.

The doctor was unable to make it out to the farm before I made my appearance, so my Grandma Isabelle accepted the responsibility for my delivery. When the doctor did arrive, he found me none the worse for wear, with a piece of shoestring tied tightly around my umbilical cord. Grandma had given me her usual coffee, which she always did with her babies. The doctor held me in his hands and pronounced my weight as seven and a half pounds, born at 6:00 p.m. Mama and Papa christened me Mary Ellen, named after my mama and my aunt Mary, Papa's half-sister. Mama's name was Mary Ellen, but most everyone called her Nellie.

Around July 4, 1918, Grandma had come to stay with us before I was born to help Mama, as she was quite ill. Mama contracted measles while teaching school as a young woman and it had affected her kidneys and eye site. My sister, Edith, was born six years before. She was born very early and was so small they didn't think she would survive. It was then the doctor told my Mama she shouldn't have any more children, as she might not live through another pregnancy and delivery.

Our house was a big, white square house with four bedrooms upstairs and one downstairs. Mama was a wonderful housekeeper and, with Edith's help, always kept the house spotless. Since Grandma had come, she cleaned the house from top to bottom, even cleaning out the milk house where the milk was separated from the cream. She worked in the garden and helped around the farm where it was needed, plus watching and playing with Edith.

My sister was used to being the only child until I came along. All the attention was on her as she was the first grandchild of both sets of grandparents. When I was born, she was happy to have a baby sister and was a big help to Mama.

After Grandma Isabelle went home, Papa's older sister, my Aunt Mary, came and stayed with us. She would bathe me on her lap, every day by the woodstove. She helped Mama with the housework and garden. She stayed until she had to go back to Canton to teach school.

Mama and Papa were so happy to have another baby and a sister for Edith to play with. However, I was a very fussy baby and cried a lot. Mama often had bad headaches and had to lie down and rest. She would say, "John, would you take Edith and Little Tyke for a while so I can get a little nap?"

Papa would take Edith by the hand as he held me and would say, "Come, Edith, let's show this little tyke what is going on outside." I usually slept through those little walks, but I think I developed a love for being outside because of them.

That next spring Papa started a Sunday School at Pleasant Ridge School, which was about one mile away. Papa, Mama, Edith, and I would bundle up and ride over to the school in the buggy. Edith sat on a little box in front of Papa and Mama while I was snug in Mama's arms. Mama was feeling better and would teach a class while I would sit on her lap. One of my first memories is sitting on her lap and playing with a necklace she wore.

As I grew, my love for the outdoors also grew. I would stand at the front window and say, "Outside, outside!"

"Edith," Mama would say, "take your little sister out and pull her in the wagon." I loved the wagon rides, but Edith tired of it way too soon. When she said, "All done," and tried to take me out of the wagon, I screamed, "No, no, outside!" So, she would reluctantly pull me around the house one more time. Mama would have to come and get me out of the wagon while I gripped the sides so tight that Edith couldn't budge me. After that, Mama would say, "It's time for your nap Mary Ellen. Now don't cry, I will rock you for a while." That was usually enough for me to quiet down and take a nap along with Mama, who needed a nap every day.

Edith really did love having a little sister, but she soon found out that I could be a pest, getting into her sewing basket and following her all over the house.

"Mama," Edith cried, "Mary Ellen will not leave me alone and she got into my sewing basket again and scattered everything all over the floor."

"Well," Mama replied, "if you learned to keep your sewing basket up where Mary Ellen can't reach, that wouldn't happen."

"But, Mama, why can't she just learn to leave my stuff alone?"

"Edith, you know that Mary Ellen is just little, she doesn't understand yet what she can have and what she can't. You have to be patient and give her one of her own toys when she wants to get into your things."

"Okay, Mama, I guess she is fun to play hide-and-seek with. She is learning where to look for me when I hide and gets so excited and squeals when she finds me."

"You're a good big sister, Edith, and a big help to me taking care of Little Tyke when I'm busy. She is a live wire for sure, always very busy investigating everything," Mama said with a chuckle.

Edith would take me out to the barn to watch Papa milk the cows. She didn't like to be out in the barn long because she didn't like the smell, and she preferred to be in the house helping Mama with the cleaning and cooking.

Papa would sing to the cows as he milked, saying, "They give more milk when I sing to them." He'd sing tunes such as "Who kicked the lantern over in Mrs. O' Leary's barn." Edith would sing along, and I would try to sing in my little voice. "Little Tyke," Papa would say, "You will learn the songs and someday you will be a good singer in the choir."

Soon it would be time to take the milk to the milk house where Mama would separate it and we would have good rich cream to put on our oatmeal each day. Mama and Papa would take the cream and butter made from the milk, along with eggs from our chickens, to town each week and trade them for other things that the family needed.

When we went to town to "trade" as Mama would say, we usually stopped by Grandpa and Grandma Sletten's house. I loved my Grandma and Grandpa. Grandpa would let me sit on his lap while he sang a song about trotting to Boston town while he bounced me up and down on his knee. "More, more!" I would cry if he stopped, until he'd start up again. Grandma always had the best sugar cookies for us too, before it would be time to go home and milk the cows again. These are some of my earliest memories.

I was born during the time my Uncle Tony, Papa's youngest brother, was in France fighting in the great war. We have old letters he wrote home to Papa talking about his experiences overseas. He knew that I had been born and couldn't wait to get back home to meet me. Sadly, he didn't get to meet me, as he died in France when I was seven months old. Edith was very close to him. He would come play with her in her playhouse, read her stories, and tell her all about his experiences in school. He even wrote to her while in France. Those letters, along with letters he had written to Papa, were kept in a special box for years to come. When Papa had to tell Edith that her Uncle Tony died in the war, she cried and cried.

Death was something that I didn't understand then, but as I grew, I soon learned about the sadness of death.

2

READY FOR SCHOOL

Edith was happy to help me learn the alphabet, and we played school together. She wasn't always very patient, but I looked up to her and admired how well she could read. The times I remember and cherish are the times we sat out under the big tree in the front yard while she read stories to me.

I knew my sister was smarter than I as she always told me that she had skipped first grade and went right into second grade. Mama had spent a lot of time teaching her at home before she started school. By the time she started at age six, she could read and was soon promoted to the second grade.

We worked together pretty well, even though I would much rather play outside than help in the house. One project our mother had us do was pick the potato bugs off the plants and place them in a can of kerosene. This was fun for me, but Edith didn't like being out in the sun that long, so I would stay out and continue picking the bugs off the plants long after she had gone in the house.

Edith and I were responsible for picking up cobs from around the corn crib and bringing them in for the cook stove in the kitchen. Mama was a wonderful cook and the smells that came from her kitchen were mouthwatering. I remember a cake she made on my fourth birthday. It was two layers and had white fluffy frosting that she beat by hand until it made peaks when she spread it on top of the cake.

Edith and I shared a bed from the time I grew out of the crib. I loved taking crackers to bed at night and munching on them. I don't recall Mama giving them to me, but somehow I was able to get them to bed with me until it became a habit of mine each night.

One night, Edith had put up with it long enough. "Mary Ellen," she said exasperated, "why do you bring those crackers to bed every night? You end up falling asleep and then they're crushed all over the bed in the morning, and I have to sleep with that! I am going to tell Mama to hide them so you can't find them."

Sheepishly I said, "I'm sorry Edith, but I just get so hungry at night and Mama doesn't let me have anything before bedtime."

"Well then," she would reply, "I will ask Mama to let you have a couple crackers before you go to bed. That will solve your problem, but you better not bring any more crackers to bed with you from now on."

Many times, Grandma and Grandpa came out to the farm for my birthday. Aunt Mary came out too, and she always had a camera and took pictures to remember the day.

Mama had a good camera too and developed her own pictures in a dark room she had set up in the upstairs bedroom closet, which had no windows and could be kept dark enough. Between Mama and Aunt Mary, I have quite a few pictures of me when I was small.

When I was three, my Grandma Isabelle died. We had been in town to visit them just a few days before. I don't remember Grandma Isabelle but have a vague memory of standing by a bed in Grandpa's house and an old lady taking hold of my hand and talking to me. I often wondered who that was. I felt it was an important part of my life, perhaps the grandma who delivered me.

Edith remembered her well, and when Papa told her that Grandma had died, she cried for days afterwards and told me about Grandma and things that she remembered. She told me many times about the day I was born, and how Grandma had taken over and delivered me when the doctor couldn't make it in time.

When I was five, a year before I started school, I had my tonsils removed. "Papa," Mama said, "Mary Ellen has constant sore throats and the doctor said she should have her tonsils removed before she starts school."

I didn't know what that was, but it didn't sound like much fun. "What are my tonsils?" I asked.

Papa said, "They are just little things you have in your mouth, and you really don't need them anyway. The doctor can remove them without much fuss."

"I'll call the doctor and make an appointment for us to bring her into the office," Mama said.

In those years, this sort of procedure was performed in the doctor's office, not the hospital. No one went to the hospital unless they were going to die. I knew that much by listening to the adults talk. They said in whispered voices, "Did you hear that Mrs. Johnson went to the hospital?" Then they shook their heads in pity for

Mrs. Johnson. I was glad I didn't have to go to the hospital to have my tonsils taken out.

The day came and we all bundled into the buggy and rode to town early in the morning after the cows were milked. Edith and I sat in front of Mama and Papa on little boxes. The horse's tails switched us in the face and we complained, but Papa didn't seem to hear our complaints. I was starting to get scared when we entered the office, and the smell was terrible. "What's that smell?" I asked Mama.

"Oh, it's just the smell of some medicine they use to help you sleep while the doctor takes your tonsils out," she reassured me.

I was happy to hear that I would just take a nap while my tonsils were removed. The doctor brought me back to the room where the deed would be done. I had to lie down on this hard table, and they put a sheet over me and a big mask over my mouth.

I started fighting and flailing my arms and legs so hard it took three people to hold me down. The next thing I remember was waking up and someone holding a wad of something in my mouth and there was blood everywhere. I started to fight again and then Papa came in and helped calm me down. "There, there, Little Tyke, you fight like a wild animal! It's all over now. Soon we can take you home and you can be in your own bed."

I later learned that I hemorrhaged and the doctor was quite concerned that I wouldn't survive the procedure. But thanks to the doctor's skill and God watching over me, I came through with flying colors.

The next fall I started school at Pleasant Ridge Country School. Edith was in eighth grade, and we walked the mile together each day unless the weather was too cold or snowy. Papa would take us in the buggy on those days. I felt so grown-up walking with Edith to school. I begged to be able to carry our lunch pail, which she was glad to let me do.

One day on our way to school, we turned the corner of the road leading to school. We just had a half mile to go. I decided to stop and set the dinner pail down while I investigated a pretty rock on the side of the road. Edith paid no attention and was in her own little world walking down the road. Suddenly, I realized that Edith was way ahead of me. I yelled out as I started running towards her. "Edith, wait for me, wait for me!"

She just continued walking and soon we were at the school yard. Edith looked at me and asked, "Where is the lunch pail?"

"I set it down at the corner and forgot it when I had to run to catch up to you," I responded. She was fuming as she went into the school to tell the teacher that she had to walk back to the corner and get the lunch pail that I had left there.

I was used to having a nap every day at home, so after lunch I would get very sleepy and have to lay my head down on my desk. The teacher was very kind and picked me up and took me to the bench in the hall and covered me up with her coat.

I loved being outside for recess. We had a merry-go-round and some chin-up bars that swung around on a single tall pole. Each child would grab hold of a bar and start running until their feet left the ground. The children continued swinging around the pole as long as they could hold on, which was not very long for some children. When they let go of their bar, it would go flying into the back of the head of the person in front of them. Many years later, it was taken down because parents complained it was unsafe. Then we got regular swings, which I enjoyed very much. I tried to see how high I could pump and sometimes I dared to jump off the swing when I was at the highest point. I thought I could fly. I often had dreams of flying over the farm.

Christmas was a wondrous time for me. I always asked Mama and Papa for things I wanted, but they would always just say, "We'll see." The Christmas I was in first grade, the teacher had us write letters to Santa Claus. Mama and Papa always told me there was no such person as Santa, which I didn't believe. Why would our teacher tell us to write a letter to someone who wasn't real? I tried to tell my teacher that my Mama and Papa said there is no Santa, but she insisted I write the letter. So, I got out my paper and pencil and started to write. I had to have the teacher help me with most of the words. I got my dolly, Matilda, the year before and now I needed a bed for her. I wrote:

Dear Santa Claus:

I am six years old. I try to be a good girl. I would like a doll cradle or a doll trunk. I wish you a Merry Christmas.

With Love,
Mary Ellen Sletten

Here is what Santa wrote back to me:

Dear Mary Ellen:

Santa will surely remember you together with all other good little girls.

Santa

I didn't know these letters were going to be printed in the Canton newspaper for all to see, including my Mama and Papa.

One day we were at Grandpa Sletten's, and he said, "Did you see Mary Ellen's writing in the newspaper this week? It was quite interesting."

Papa said, "No, we haven't gotten the paper yet this week. Do you have yours handy?"

Grandpa retrieved his paper from the table and gave it to Papa. I had no idea what Grandpa was talking about until Papa found the letter and read it out loud. I was worried he was going to punish me, but he just read it out loud, then threw back his head and laughed. "That is quite a letter Mary Ellen. When did you write this?

"Our teacher *made* us write it, Papa. I didn't want to." I answered timidly.

"Well, I know you don't believe in Santa. You know God gave you your Mama and me who love you so much that we buy gifts for you," Papa said as he put the paper down.

That Christmas there was a doll cradle under the little tree in our dining room. Now Matilda didn't have to sleep on a pillow on the floor by my bed anymore.

That first year of school was swell for me. I had friends I knew from Sunday School, and I loved having my sister there to watch out for me. She came to my defense if anyone teased me. The next year I found to be totally different as Edith went to high school in Canton.

THE NEW CAR
1924

THE YEAR I ENTERED school was 1924, and there were two close calls with the horses. Mama saw many people were getting new cars and she thought they were so much safer than horse-and-buggy.

The first incident happened one summer Sunday after church. We were invited to the Anderson's for lunch. Mama, Edith, and I were to ride home in the Anderson's car, and Papa would take the horse-and-buggy home, do the chores, and then join us for supper.

This was my first real car ride. It was so big, and Edith and I sat on little fold-down seats in the back. We had a wonderful time at the Anderson's, and they soon started getting ready for our supper. It was common to stay for the day and enjoy both dinner and supper. When the supper was ready, we all began to look for Papa.

"He should have been done with the chores by now," Mama said. "I hope nothing is wrong."

Mr. Anderson was about to take his car over and see why Papa was late, when Papa drove his team of horses into the yard. He had quite a story to tell us about his trip home after church.

"We were going along nicely, and I was enjoying the ride when all of a sudden, the horses were spooked by something. They took off like a shot. It was all I could do to keep them on the straight and narrow way. They ran about a mile past the farm before I got them stopped. Boy, was I sweating! I think they got running out of their system."

"John," Mama exclaimed, "I don't know why we don't get a car. They are so much safer than the horses."

"That's for sure," Mr. Anderson added. "When you want to stop, you just step on the brake and you stop. Horses can be very unpredictable and head strong, wanting to go where they want to go and not where you want them to go."

The second incident happened one day when Papa and I were going to pick up Aunt Jennie, Mama's sister, who was coming to visit us from Hartington, Nebraska, as she often did.

We were riding along when all of a sudden, the horses started running. Faster and faster and faster they went. I hung on tight because I was afraid I would be thrown out of the buggy. Papa was hollering, "Whoa, whoa!" His arms were straining to keep them under control. But the horses would not stop. Suddenly, the tongue connecting the carriage to the horses broke in two, snapped back, and its sharp end flew back and pierced the back of the buggy between Papa's head and mine. By that time, the horses had run away, and I was bawling and tightly hanging on. When the buggy came to a sudden stop, I was almost thrown out of the buggy.

Papa was very shaken when he looked the situation over. We were close to a neighbor's farmhouse and Papa said, "Mary Ellen, run back to DeNures' and stay there." Papa went to catch the horses on foot. It was after that incident he made the decision to buy a car.

When I got to the neighbors, I was so scared I couldn't talk. Finally, after I had stopped crying, I was able to tell them what happened.

We somehow were able to pick up Aunt Jennie and get back home. Again, Mama wished we had a car. Papa agreed with her.

Soon Papa cashed in the Liberty Bond he had bought during the war and bought a Model T. He went into town one day to pick it up. Edith and I were so excited to see our new car. We waited in our little playhouse, which was in a corner of the yard by the road. We had strung twine from one fence to another and hung an old peach box on the corner post, which was the cupboard for storing our kitchen supplies and pies. We waited and waited, making mud pies as we waited. Edith really didn't like making mud pies any-more, but she helped me that day to make the time go by faster. We wanted to see Papa as he came up over the small rise in the road.

Suddenly, we heard a horn. "Aooga, aooga." There was Papa coming down the road so proud in the new car. He was going along at quite a clip and when he came to the driveway, he turned a little too soon and was going a little too fast, striking the corner post and knocking our cupboard down. Both Edith and I jumped back, but as Papa looked like he had it under control going down the driveway, we followed cheering, "Yay, Yay!" That post always leaned a little after that.

Mama had come out of the house to see the commotion. Papa had made a small ramp out of dirt going up into the old shed so he could easily drive the car in. He had slowed just before the shed and was lightly giving the car gas to get up into the shed. He kept pressing the gas and all of a sudden, the car lurched forward into the shed and right out the back wall. Papa was hollering the whole time, "Whoa, whoa!" But the horse with tires didn't whoa. He spent the rest of that day repairing the back wall of the shed.

Edith and I had to dust the car every Saturday so it would be clean and shiny for our trip to Sunday school the next day. We got up early to get ready. Mama, Edith, and I wore our best Sunday hats.

"John," Mama said one of the first Sundays we took our car to church. "Can we have the side curtains on today? If we don't have them on, our hats will blow off."

Papa loved to have all the curtains off when we went anywhere unless it was threatening to rain. I loved it that way too. The breezes felt so exhilarating going down the road. We could go so much faster than the horses did, and we didn't have to look at the back end of a horse anymore and be switched with their tails. He would usually consent to at least put the back curtain in, which helped.

One fourth of July we were traveling to Beresford, which was about thirteen miles away. Papa wanted the curtains off, as it was a beautiful day. We had only gone about two miles when Edith's hat blew off. "Papa, stop, my hat blew off!" Edith cried.

Papa came to a stop and said, "Edith, you have to hang on to your hat. Jump down now and go back and get it."

Edith ran back and retrieved her hat. I was glad that I had a string that went under my chin so I didn't have to hang on to my hat.

Mary Ellen (left) with her cousin Bernice Depue, playing with dolls.
About age four, circa 1922

PLAYMATES AND COUSINS
1924

MOST OF MY PLAYMATES were from Pleasant Ridge, the grade school I attended and where we had Sunday school and church each week. Our home was about a mile from the small white school house. I remember going to church excited about playing outside with my friends. Sometimes Mama and Papa packed a lunch, and we stayed after church and had a picnic.

One Sunday in mid-July, I helped Mama pack the picnic basket with food for our family. "Mama," I asked, "will my friend Mable be there today?"

"I expect their family will be in church today as they usually are, but Mary Ellen, you have to remember to sit quietly during church and listen to the preacher," Mama warned.

That was always a hard thing for me to do. I loved looking out the windows at the green trees swaying in the breeze, and I could imagine being out there running and playing with my friends.

I was having a hard time sitting still in church that day as I wanted to get down off the hard bench and run outside to play. I would squirm and try to get down and stand by Mama, but she would have none of it. "Mary Ellen," Mama said sternly, "you have to be still!" She plopped me down on the bench again. I just couldn't sit still. I felt like I had something telling me, "It will be so wonderful to be outside instead of in this stuffy church."

Finally, Mama took my arm firmly and I was escorted outside. Oh, I had a feeling of joy at being outside, but that joy soon turned to regret. "Mary Ellen," Mama said sternly, "I have told you that you must sit still in church, and you have continued to disobey me." As she led me to the small grove of trees, I knew what my fate was going to be.

"Mama, please don't spank me. I was just getting tired of sitting so long." But she was not to be deterred. She found a small switch, which she broke off from a tree, and I received my due punishment.

When church was finally over, I was free to run and play with the other children until the picnic dinner was arranged on long tables brought from the school. We filled our plates with food and sat on the grass or on the swings, which never turned out well, as the swing would move at the wrong time and our dinners would end upside down in the dirt.

I loved to climb, and as I got a little bigger, I tried to climb trees. One time my cousin Kermit, who was about six years older than me, came to visit us. He loved climbing trees and would get way up in the treetops. Oh, how I wanted to do that.

"Come on, Mary Ellen," he would say. "Follow me and I will help you get up into the treetops. You can see all over the place from there."

I was a little scared, but he encouraged me all the way. Soon I was sitting on a branch way up in the tree and we were happily looking at the view from there.

"Wow, Kermit! This is way up in the sky! I think I better get down before Papa finds me and scolds me for climbing so high."

"Okay, Mary Ellen, just follow me as we go down and you will be safe and sound on the ground before you know it."

Kermit started down, but I was too scared to let go of the branch I was clinging to. "I can't! I can't!" I screamed down to him as he descended the tree. "Go get Papa."

Soon Kermit was back with Papa, and I was scared I would get a switching for sure.

"Hey, Little Tyke, what are you doing up in that tree with all the birds? Are you pretending to be Zacchaeus?" Papa teased. I knew the story about Zacchaeus in the Bible, who was so short that he couldn't see over all the people, so he climbed up into a tree to see Jesus passing by.

Soon Papa had climbed up to where I was and told me he would stay right behind me and not let me fall. "Listen to me and just take each step as I tell you to. You will soon be on the ground safe and sound."

So, that is what I did. Papa said, "Now put your foot on this branch and bring your hand down to this branch. That's the way, you are doing great."

When we got down, I began to cry uncontrollably, partially because I had been so scared and partially because I knew I had done wrong and would suffer the consequences. But Papa just took me in his arms and held me tight. "There, there, Little Tyke, it's okay now. Just remember this the next time you try to do things that you are too little to do." He also gave Kermit a little talking to for letting me climb up so high with him.

I loved it when my cousin, Bernice, came to visit. Her Mama, Maggie, was a sister to my Mama. Bernice was only about seven months younger than I was and we were about the same size. They lived in Hartington, Nebraska, where our Grandpa and Grandma Bixby lived. They would come on the train to see us. One time when they were visiting, Mama sewed Bernice and me new dresses.

"Mama, can you take a picture of us playing with our dolls in our new dresses?" I asked.

Mama was good at taking pictures and she developed them in the upstairs closet, which was very dark. I never entered that closet as Mama told me never to go in there, as it might let light in and ruin pictures she was developing. Besides, I was scared to go into a dark closet.

This was our usual conversation when Bernice and I played "dollies."

Bernice would hold her dolly up and say, "Patty, you must be a good girl and eat all your beans." Then she would place her in my little highchair and proceed to feed her dolly. "That's a good girl," Bernice said. "My, what a big girl you are getting to be!"

I would pretend to change my dolly's diaper while she was feeding Patty. When it was my turn to use the highchair, I placed little Matilda in the chair and proceeded to feed her. "I know you love apple sauce," I would say to Matilda. "Yum, yummm!"

After we fed our babies, we took them for a ride in the buggy. We took turns pushing the buggy and talking about the trials we had with our children. Bernice and her brothers and mother would come to visit and stay for a week at a time, but before long her Mama and Papa moved farther away, and she didn't get to visit much anymore.

Bernice had an older brother, Eugene, who was two years older than me. Mama once said, "Eugene is such a cute baby, but Aunt Maggie had some problem when he was born, which caused him to have some difficulties." I didn't understand that, but Mama seemed to know about it. He never went to school, as it was common for parents to keep students with disabilities home, but I could tell his Mama loved him very much. She would dress him up in cute clothes and take him everywhere. He was a very happy sweet boy.

Bernice also had a younger brother, Henry, who was three years younger than her. He was a cute baby, but didn't seem to do what other babies do, like sitting up by himself or learning to crawl at a certain age. I didn't get to know him, because they moved farther away before he was three. I later learned that Henry also had learning problems and only attended school through first grade.

The other cousin I loved was Elmer Bixby. His father was my Mama's brother, Benjamin. Their family came to the farm to visit when the children were younger, and I loved playing with Elmer. He was three years younger than me, so I showed him all around the farm. He loved playing with me at the farm as their family lived in Sioux City, Nebraska and had not experienced farm life.

"Elmer," I said with authority, "let's go see if the mama pigs have had their babies." I loved the baby pigs when they were born, and the mama pigs let me come in with them and scratch their bellies.

Elmer was mesmerized as I took a baby pig from the mother and brought it out for him to hold. "See, Elmer, they are just like human babies. They love to be held and rocked. Do you want to hold one?"

"No!" Elmer said. "They are too dirty! My Mama said I should not go near those dirty pigs."

"They aren't dirty. See, just as pink and nice as can be," I replied.

Life on the farm was, for the most part, an adventure every day. When Edith and I were old enough, we helped Papa make hay. Edith backed the hay rack up to the stack with a team of horses, and Papa pitched the hay up on top. I would be up on the stack and move the hay around where Papa directed me.

We also walked behind Papa when he cut grain and stacked it into shocks, keeping the grain heads off the ground by creating upright stacks in a circle. It was a hot and tiresome job that required a lot of walking.

I much preferred working outside with Papa, so when Mama said, "Mary Ellen, it's your turn to wipe the dishes today," as Edith began washing the dishes after a meal, I had an excuse ready.

"I have to go to the bathroom first," I said, and out the door I went to the sanctuary of the outhouse. I loved the outhouse, as it was a good place to think and plan things I could do that day. There was also a Sears and Roebuck catalog out there, and I would pour over it, dreaming about what I might get for Christmas. As usual, time got away from me, and by the time I went into the house, Edith had the dishes all washed and dried, as she couldn't stand to let them sit there waiting for me.

Life for me was one adventure after another, and with my imagination, I thought up many adventures.

5

EARLY SCHOOL YEARS

School was one big adventure for me. Not because I was soaking up all the knowledge the teacher had for us, but because I lived for recess and playing with my school chums. It was hard for me to concentrate on the teacher when all I could do was stare out the window and wish I was outside instead.

Second grade was especially hard for me, as my sister Edith was not there to help me. She had started high school in Canton and was staying in town during the week. I didn't realize how much I would miss her. The worst was at night, sleeping all alone in our bed. I would cry many nights, wishing she was there. I never told Mama and Papa how lonely I was, and I didn't tell Edith either.

I still got teased at school, and Edith was not there to defend me. I learned fast how to defend myself.

Before I started second grade, Mama made me a book bag to carry my lunch pail and the books I needed to bring home. "Now, Mary Ellen," she instructed me, "don't put too many books in the bag or it will get too heavy to carry home, and don't put every rock and pinecone you find on the way home in there either." I was still quite small, and she thought having one bag to carry would be easier for me.

I usually did find some treasured rocks along the way, and I couldn't help but pick them up and take them home.

There was one neighbor boy who especially caused me grief. His name was Russell, and he teased me incessantly. One day I was walking home minding my own business when he came up behind me and tried to pull my hair.

"Russell!" I shouted. "If you try to touch me, I will hit you with my book bag!" Knowing I had several rocks in the bag plus my metal dinner pail, I thought it would scare him off.

"You don't scare me, Mary Ellen Sletten," he retorted. "You're so little, you couldn't scare a fly."

At that, I took my bag, wound it up, and swung it around my head. He didn't get out of the way soon enough and I hit him square on the side of his head. He went crying down the road to his house. I felt proud for defending myself, even though I knew Mama and Papa wouldn't be happy that I hit someone.

One day Russell rode his horse to school, as many students did in those days. As I was walking along, I heard a horse coming up behind me. I glanced back and saw it was Russell. He kept coming closer and closer and looked like he was going to run over me. I lifted my book bag thinking he would not mess with me again.

"Russell!" I shouted. "You better get over on the other side of the road!" I knew he had the upper hand being on his horse, but I stood my ground.

As he came next to me, his horse stepped on my shoe and broke the strap. He didn't hurt my foot, but when I got home, I showed Papa what happened to my shoe. He immediately walked to Russell's house and showed his father my damaged shoe. After that Russell didn't bother me much, and school days were a little more pleasant.

I was good at thinking of things to do during school recess. One day I said to my friend, Mable, "Let's go play in the sand that's out back by the outhouses." We didn't have anything to use to dig in the sand, so I suggested we use our shoes. They worked great to dig, and we put sand in them to dump into big piles. Then I suggested we pour sand down the outhouse hole. We took shoe load after shoe load to the outhouse and poured the sand in a stream down the hole.

When the bell rang, we hurriedly were pounding our shoes to get the sand out of them. You can guess what happened next. One of my shoes dropped down into the hole. I immediately began to cry as we ran towards the school.

"What on earth is the matter?" the teacher asked as we ran into the school. I was crying so hard I couldn't tell her.

Mable explained, "We had sand in our shoes, so we were dumping it out in the outhouse when Mary Ellen's shoe dropped in the hole."

Of course, all the children were in from recess and heard the whole story. They all began to laugh, Russell the loudest. My volume of crying rose to a fevered pitch.

"Don't worry, Mary Ellen," the teacher said sympathetically. "I think I can retrieve it. Let's go out and see what we can do." After she asked one of the older girls to keep order in the school, we made our way to the outhouse. Along the way she stopped at a grove of trees and found a long branch.

All the while I was thinking about what Mama would say about losing my shoe in the outhouse. Shoes cost a lot of money, and Mama and Papa always told us to take good care of our shoes and clothes because they would have to do until we outgrew them. I had visions of wearing a pair of my old shoes to school the rest of the school year even though they were too small for me.

The teacher was skilled at reclaiming things from the outhouse hole. She had clearly recovered other treasures that had accidentally fell into the hole. She was able to use the branch to hook the shoe and raise it up and out of the hole. And it was not too bad, as it had landed sole-side down so the top was pretty clean still. She helped me clean it off at the water pump, and it was good as new. Another spanking averted!

When you attend a country school, a favorite game at recess was playing softball. I wanted to play so bad, but because I was small, I rarely got to play. Two people would take turns picking who they wanted on their team. I was usually the last to be picked and they would say unenthusiastically, "I guess I'll take Mary Ellen." The rule was that everyone had to be included.

I would skip over to where my team was standing and await my turn to bat. If my turn came up, I immediately would strike out. Usually, I was placed way out in the outfield where no balls ever came. Most of the time I would play in the dirt and not pay attention to the game. When one of the bigger boys would hit a home run, everyone would shout and jump up and down. I would follow along and do the same, but I had no clue what had happened.

When winter came, Papa would crank up the Model T and take me to and from school each day. I missed the horse drawn sleigh in the winter. I loved being pulled in the sleigh by the horses after Papa fastened Grandpa Sletten's old sleigh bells to their harnesses. The horses lifted their feet up high and pranced all the way with the bells ringing merrily. When the weather was mild, I could walk, but if there was a storm threatening, then school was called off and I got to stay home.

Mama always had things she wanted me to do, which kept me busy. She would say, "Mary Ellen, today we're going to clean your room. It looks like a tornado went through there."

I would respond, "Mama, do we have to? It is so cold up there in the winter. That's why my clothes are on the floor. At night I have to quick take off my clothes and hop right into bed. Sometimes I take the clothes I plan on wearing the next day under the covers with me so they will be nice and warm to get into in the morning."

When Edith was here, she would pick up my clothes and put them away so our room was always neat and clean.

"Mary Ellen, you must learn to keep your room tidy. Some day you will be going off to high school, and the people you board with will not like you having a messy room." I didn't think I would ever be that old, but I learned to do what Mama told me and as I got older, I managed to keep my room neat. When Edith came home on the weekend, she was impressed that I kept our room neat and tidy.

We had a lot of fun memories of days when we were "snowed in." Papa would make popcorn on the woodstove, and then he would read stories to us as we sat by the warm fire.

When Edith came home on the weekend, she would tell me all about going to high school. "It's a very big place with lots of stairs to climb and many rooms where our classes are held. It is a little hard at first to find the right room, but you get used to it."

I couldn't imagine having more than one room in school. I would surely get lost in a big building like that. Oh well, I thought, it will be a long time before I get old enough to go to high school.

Mary Ellen with her grampa, Ingvold Sletten,
on her sixth birthday, circa 1924

MEMORIES OF MY GRANDPARENTS

I DON'T REMEMBER MY FATHER'S mother, Isabelle Sletten, who delivered me. I was only three when she passed away. I learned a lot about her through my father and my aunts Mary and Ellen. The stories they told about growing up sounded like a page out of history. I used to ask my Grandpa Sletten, "What was it like to live in the 'olden days'?"

He would recount stories about the time he and his family came from Wisconsin on a wagon train.

"Did you see any Indians"? I asked with wide eyes.

"Well, no Indians, but we saw plenty of wild animals in the wilderness we had to travel through," he teased.

I was fascinated with the 'olden times' and loved the stories about Danial Boone and Wild Bill Hickok.

"What did you do without a telephone in your house? How did you call someone you needed to talk to?" I asked one day.

"We relied on letters, which took quite a while to reach the person. If we needed to contact a neighbor, we just rode over to their place and talked to them," Grandpa said. "We also had the telegraph, but you had to go to town to send it. The telegraph was much faster than a letter. Someday, people won't know anything about the telegraph or letters."

"I like writing letters," I said proudly. "Letters are good because you can save them and read them over and over. You can't do that with a telephone call."

"That's for sure, Little Tyke. You keep writing letters. If you write to me, I will save every one so I can read them over and over," Grandpa said.

"Okay, Grandpa, I will write to you every week. That way, we can keep in touch when I can't come to see you."

At that, he pulled me onto his lap and gave me a whiskery kiss on my cheek. At some point I decided that I was too old to sit on Grandpa's lap, but he asked for a hug every time we saw him, and he snuck a whisker-rub on my face. I laughed and said, "Grandpa, you need to shave!" He threw back his head and laughed and laughed.

He was such a jolly grandpa, and he always made a story about everything. I remember he could sit on the floor and put his leg behind his head. I tried and tried to do this, but I never could. He could also stand flat-footed on the floor and lean over to put the palms of his hands flat on the floor without bending his knees. Even though he had asthma, he was very active and helped Papa a lot on the farm. He loved to garden and had a huge garden in Canton for many years. Every summer he would take the produce from his garden to sell on the street corner downtown. He made a little money that way and got to keep up on the news around town also. Grandpa was never one to sit around doing nothing. He always kept busy.

Grandpa was a good cook too. When we went to see him, he made French toast. I loved his French toast and ate quite a few pieces.

Mama said, "Mary Ellen, I sometimes wonder if you have hollow legs for all you can eat!" Grandpa laughed at that, saying, "It doesn't look like she is slowing down much," and he kept making more for me.

Grandpa was very caring and always tried to help people out when they were down on their luck. One time he took a whole family of seven into his home when they had no place to go. He felt if he had abundance, he should share it with others. He always had plenty to feed them with his big garden, and soon the family was able to move to a place of their own.

Grandpa always went to church, and I loved sitting next to him with Mama, Papa, Edith and my Aunt Mary. Sometimes we went to his house after church, or he came home with us. That didn't happen often, as I think he didn't want to ask Papa to take him back home before chore time. When he finally got a car of his own, he would proudly drive out to the farm, staying under the thirty miles per hour limit. He said he liked going slow so he could look at all the crops in the fields as he went by. "It's still faster than a horse-and-buggy," he said.

Mama's parents, Chauncey and Eliza Belle Bixby, lived in Hartington, Nebraska. I did know them, but not as well as my Grandpa Sletten.

"Mama, Mama," I called as I saw Grandpa and Grandma Bixby drive into the yard. "Grandma and Grandpa Bisby are here!"

"It's *Bixby*," Edith said, "like 'bix' and bee together!"

I had a little trouble saying Bixby, but I was happy they came to see us. We didn't see them very much, but when they came Mama was especially happy and had cleaned the house top to bottom. Grandpa Bixby was a little scary to me as he had a gruff, stern look to him, so different from my other grandpa. Grandma Bixby was a warm, jolly lady and always laughed at things I would say or do. She didn't have much of a lap to sit on, but she was soft and smelled like flowers.

I liked listening to Grandma and Mama talk about when Mama was growing up. She always had stories about Mama that she hadn't told me before. Mama was the oldest of her six siblings, so she was the one who helped Grandma with the other children and the housework. Even though everyone called my mama Nellie, Grandma would always call her Mary Ellen. I liked the way she said "Mary Ellen." She said my name the same way, and it made me feel so important that my name was the same as Mama's.

"Mary Ellen, I believe this little Mary Ellen has grown a foot since the last time we were here," she would say as she fussed over me. "She and Edith remind me of when your sisters were little. We had three girls before we got our first boy." Mama's sisters, Edith, Edna, and Jennie, were still not married and lived with Grandpa and Grandma. Sometimes they came with them when they visited us, but this time they stayed home.

Grandpa Bixby loved to tell stories too. He always made the most of his stories, and I liked when he talked about the time Papa lived with them when he taught at the school that was close to the Bixby farm.

"You were pretty sweet on Nellie, John. I remember you asked if you could go pick up Nellie from her school on Friday and bring her home," Grandpa said. "I was happy to have you do that and so was Nellie's brother, Benjamin. I remember one time I asked Benjamin to hitch up the buggy so that when John was out of school, he could go straight to get Nellie. Well, Ben thought he would have some fun with John, so he hitched up a very spirited horse to the buggy. John had quite a ride to Nellie's school with that horse, but by the time he got there, the horse had settled down and he and Nellie had a nice ride home."

Mama and Papa looked at each other and laughed and laughed. "Ben never did that again!" Papa said. "I had a little talking to him when we got home and heard what happened."

Even though I always liked seeing my Grandma and Grandpa Bixby come to visit, I was a little relived when they went home again. I just didn't see them very much, so I didn't get to know them very well. I was grateful I got to know them a little, as Grandma Bixby died in 1927 when I was eight years old. I remember going to the funeral and thought Grandpa looked so sad and lost without Grandma. Grandpa had his daughters, Edith, Edna, and Jennie to care for him after Grandma died.

About a month after Grandma Bixby died, Mama's sister Edna died. This was very hard for Mama as she was close to Edna, being only eighteen months older than her. Edna had a lot of health problems and was sick quite a lot. The last time she went in the hospital, she died from a blood clot after surgery. Mama cried a lot, and we made the sad trip to Hartington for her funeral. Now only Grandpa, Aunt Edith and Aunt Jennie were together in their house in Hartington.

After Grandma and Aunt Edna passed away, Grandpa Bixby came to stay with us for a while. He slept in a bedroom upstairs. One morning I was up and ready to go downstairs to see what Mama had fixed for breakfast. As I passed Grandpa's room, I noticed the door was open and Grandpa was still lying in bed. "Come here, Mary Ellen," he said. "Just come and lie down by me for a little while." That scared me and I ran as fast as I could down the stairs to my Mama. I had never told my Mama how I felt about Grandpa Bixby or how I was afraid of him. But this morning as I rushed into the kitchen, Mama asked me what I was in such a hurry for.

"Mama," I said breathlessly, "Grandpa wanted me to lie in bed with him this morning, I just said no and ran downstairs."

Mama just said, "Mary Ellen, you did the right thing by coming and telling me about it. Grandpa is very lonely and sad now that Grandma and Edna are gone. Since you haven't spent much time around him, you feel shy. That's normal and I think Grandpa understands. I'll talk to him about it."

One thing I remember about going to Grandpa Bixby's house is that he loved cats and had several in his house. I loved that, but Mama and Papa always said that "cats belonged outside, not in the house" so we never had any house cats. He also had a lot of flowers in his garden, and he said Grandma always cared for them. He let me pick some for Aunt Edna's funeral, and I put them on her casket at the cemetery. She is buried next to her mama and her little brother, Edward, who died when he was only one year old.

I always thought that story was so sad. One morning Grandpa and Grandma got up and found him dead in his crib. When I looked at little Edward's grave, I tried to imagine a little baby boy lying in the ground. It sent shivers up my back and made me want to cry. To me, life should always be about happy times, not sad, but Papa told me sometimes we must have sad times so we appreciate the good times. It did make me appreciate my Mama, who was not that much older than Edna. Mama was sick a lot, and sometimes I thought that maybe she would die too. This scared me, so I always tried to appreciate having her with us and tried to do all I could to make life easier for her. I learned at an early age that life can end at any time and that we should love those around us while we have them.

The Measles Outbreak

"Mama, mama," I called down the stairs between fits of coughing. "Mama, I don't feel good." Then I slipped back to my warm bed and bundled up because of the terrible chills. Edith was coughing too and lay hot next to me.

"What is it, Mary Ellen?" Mama said as she entered our room. She put her cool hand on my forehead, and it felt so nice. "Why, Mary Ellen, you are burning up with fever," and then she checked Edith and said the same thing. "Let me light a lamp so I can get a better look at you both."

It was late summer, and school was to start in a couple of weeks. Mama brought the kerosine lamp close to our bed and pulled the covers down so she could see more than my nose peeking out from under the covers.

"Oh, no!" Mama exclaimed. "Why, you both have the measles!" The word "measles" struck fear in Mama as she knew the damage having the measles could do and she also knew that Papa's brother, Thomas, died from having the measles. "I will have Papa call the doctor to come out and check you over. I don't like that cough either. Now, you both stay bundled up in bed until the doctor comes. I will bring you some nice warm soup and some bread and jam."

"Mama," Edith said as she pulled her head out from under the covers. "Will we die because we have the measles? I sure hope I can start school again in two weeks because I don't want to get behind."

"Of course, you won't die; a lot of people get the measles and don't die. Papa had them when his brother did, and he turned out fine," she said. "Now, try to get a little sleep, and I'll be back up in about half an hour with your breakfast."

"Mama," I said weakly, "I love you."

"I love you too," Mama said as she went out the door and down the steps.

"Edith, are you afraid of dying?" I asked.

"Oh, Mary Ellen, we aren't going to die! When the doctor gets here, he will take care of us and not let us die."

"But you do hear of people dying when they have the measles. How do you know that we won't die?" I asked.

Edith turned to me and took my hand. "Mama and Papa wouldn't let us die. I know Papa will pray for us too, Mary Ellen. Now, try to sleep a little."

We both dozed off for a while when Mama came into our room with the good-smelling soup and fresh bread with jam. I perked up a little at the thought of Mama's good bread and homemade jam. But when I tried to sit up, I got a little dizzy and had to lie back down. "Mama, my head hurts so bad, I don't know if I can eat anything."

"Mary Ellen, just try to eat what you can. Here is a pitcher of cool water for you to drink. Edith, will you help Mary Ellen eat something?" Mama said turning to Edith.

"I'll try Mama," Edith replied, "but I don't know if I can make her eat, as I don't feel much like eating either. My head is splitting, and now I am so hot, where a half hour ago I was freezing. When will the doctor be here?"

"Papa called him, and he will be here as soon as possible, but you know he has other people he needs to help too. He said he would try to get here before noon. He told us to keep you in bed and make sure you take in fluids, so if you can't eat, at least drink some water," Mama said.

"Mama," I said softly, "can you stay here and read to us? I like hearing your voice."

"What do you want me to read?"

"How about a story about the olden days?" I said.

"Well, I think Papa would be better at telling stories about the olden days," Mama said. "I'll read something from a book that Edith had, and then when Papa has the chores done, he can come up and tell you a story about the olden days."

Mama read to us until we had fallen asleep again, then quietly tiptoed out of the room and back downstairs.

Papa was in the kitchen washing up. "How are our two girlies with measles?" he asked.

"I think they will be fine, but they are feeling pretty rough. They both have bad headaches, and now they are coughing terribly,"

Mama said. "I hope it's not whooping cough. That will make things even worse. Edith is worried about school starting in two weeks, but I think Mary Ellen is happy to be able to stay home a few more weeks. Mary Ellen wants you to come up and tell her a story about the olden days when you can."

"Let's have a little breakfast and then I can go up before I head out to the field," Papa said. "I think they need to rest as much as they can. I'll be happy when the doctor gets here; maybe he has something to help with their headaches and fever."

After Mama and Papa had finished their breakfast, they both went up the stairs to Edith and Mary Ellen's room and quietly tiptoed in. Both were sound asleep, so they quietly returned to the kitchen.

"I better get out to the field. Sam is coming over to help me today," Papa said as he gave Mama a little kiss.

About eleven o'clock the doctor drove into our yard. Mama told him about our symptoms and when they had started. Then she brought him up to our room. We both woke up as the door creaked open and when I saw the doctor, I hid my head under the covers. "I don't want medicine! It's icky!"

"Oh, Mary Ellen," the doctor said calmly, "if you need to have medicine to get well, don't you want that?"

"I suppose," I said as I peeked out from under the covers.

The doctor took our temperatures and looked at all the spots we had on our bodies. Then he looked in our throats and made us gag. He listened to our chests with his cold hearing tool. I think it is called a stethoscope, but I can't say that word.

"Well," the doctor finally said, "You both have a pretty good case of the measles, and I think by the sound of your coughs, you probably have whooping cough as well." The doctor turned towards Mama and addressed her. "It's just hard to tell what the effects of this may be until we see how they recover. I'll leave something that will help with the fever and cough."

The doctor instructed the girls, "I want you both to stay in bed for the next few days. Drink a lot of water and try to eat, even though it may be hard as your throats look pretty red. It will be a couple of pretty rough days ahead, but I'll come out on Thursday and see how you're doing."

"Thank you, doctor," Mama said. Before he left, he gave us each a dose of medicine, and then Mama led him out the door and down the stairs.

"Edith," I asked, "I wonder if the doctor was telling the truth or if we're more sicker than we think."

"Mary Ellen, it's sicker, not more sicker. Don't worry about it. I'm sure we'll both be back to normal and back to school in two weeks."

"I think I'll take more than two weeks to get better 'cause I don't care if I go back to school just yet," I replied.

"Okay, but let's have another glass of water and try to sleep some more. The medicine the doctor gave us is making me feel sleepy, but my headache is a little better."

We both turned over and were soon fast asleep.

The next thing I knew, Mama was shaking me awake and said, "Mary Ellen, its suppertime and you have been sleeping all day. You must get up and use the pot now, then I'll bring up some supper for you and Edith."

When Mama pulled the covers off me, my night gown was soaking wet. "Mama, I wet the bed," I said, shocked at the fact.

"No, Mary Ellen, your fever has broken and that makes you sweat. I'll get you a clean nightie and change the sheets so you have a nice dry bed to get into," Mama said.

I was happy that I hadn't wet the bed. It had been a long time since I did that, but I remember Mama was worried that I'd still be wetting my bed by the time I started school. Edith was happy too when I didn't wet the bed anymore. I remember her calling out to Mama, "Mama, Mary Ellen wet the bed again!" Then Mama would have to come upstairs and change my nightie and sheets. I knew it was added work for Mama, and that she would likely have to wash sheets again the next day.

After Mama changed our bedsheets and we were both in dry nighties again, she went downstairs to get us some supper. I was a little hungry now and wondered what wonderful meal Mama would bring to us. Edith was sitting up and trying to comb her hair and fussing about the spots she had on her face.

"Oh, Edith," I teased, "are you worried that the boys won't like you with all the spots you have? Look, I said as I pulled my nightie up. I have more than you do!"

"Well, I'm not going to pull my nightie up for you to see how many I have. I just hope that these spots are all gone before I have to go back to school."

Soon I heard the steps creaking and I knew Mama had our supper, but I was surprised to see Papa at the door. "Papa, Papa, "I squealed, "You came to see us!"

"I sure did, Little Tyke," Papa said. "I couldn't stay away any longer. Besides, I hear you want a story about the olden days."

"Well, what did you bring us to eat?" I asked as my stomach began to grumble. "Then you can tell us a story while we eat."

"Well, it looks like Mama made you some nice soup again and some apple sauce, which I know you like. The doctor said to go easy on solids until you are up and around. I tried to get her to put a piece of homemade apple pie on your tray, but she wouldn't budge on that. So, she gave you sauce instead."

"I would have liked pie," I said sadly.

"Maybe in a couple of days, Mary Ellen," Papa said. "Now eat up and I will tell you about a time when I was a little boy."

As we ate, we were entranced by Papa's story.

"When I was about your age, Mary Ellen, I got really sick and the doctor came to see me. He said that I had pneumonia and there was nothing he could do for me. He told my Mama and Papa that I may die. Of course, Mama and Papa cried to think that they might lose a little boy. I would be the fourth boy that Mama had lost, and she cried and cried. Well, I heard what the doctor said outside my room, and I said to myself, *I will not die!*

"Did you live?" I asked without thinking.

"Mary Ellen, he wouldn't be here telling us the story if he had died," Edith said exasperated.

"Yes, with Mama and Papa's fine care, I recovered. But I had been so sick for so long that I had to learn to walk all over again," Papa said.

"You mean, like a baby?" I asked.

"Yes, your Aunt Mary had to help me walk around until I was strong enough to walk on my own, but I was soon back to my normal self. My Mama and Papa prayed that I would get better, and your Mama and I have prayed for you girls to be strong and get well soon," Papa said.

"I believe God hears our prayers and will help us to get better," I said.

When we were finished with our supper, Papa helped us get settled in bed and he gave each of us a kiss on the forehead. I felt so comforted when Papa was there. I knew he would do whatever was needed to keep us safe.

By the time Thursday came and the doctor came out to look us over, we were much better and the spots seemed to be fading. He told us we could be up but not too active and to take it easy.

"Does that mean that we don't have to do the dishes or help Mama clean?" I asked hopefully.

"Well, for a few days anyway, then you can do things that you feel able to do. Remember, your Mama needs help too, so do what you can to help her."

"I will," said Edith.

"I will too," I said, mimicking Edith's response. Even though I didn't like to do the dishes, I would try to help.

Within a week we were both so much better, and the spots were almost gone. Mama and Papa thought it would be okay for us to start school the next week, and I was feeling a little more ready to go back, as I missed my friends.

Being sick is no fun, I decided. I hoped that I would not have any more bad sickness again, and that all our family would stay healthy—especially Mama, as she was sick more and more of the time.

Family picture (left to right): John Sletten, Mary Ellen Sletten, Mary Ellen (Nellie) Sletten, Edith Sletten, circa 1920

MAMA

My mama worked so hard even though she suffered a lot of physical problems. She had the measles as a young woman when she was teaching school. Because of that, her eyesight was affected as well as her kidneys and heart. She suffered terrible headaches and a lot of swelling in her legs and feet.

She loved her garden, even though it was hard work planting and weeding it. Papa and Edith helped. When I got big enough, I would help too.

"Mama," I said one day. "Why do we need this huge garden for just four people?"

Mama answered, "Mary Ellen, it is good for people to store up things we need because some year we might not be able to grow a garden. Just like the squirrels—they don't just eat what they need for the day. They are always storing food for the winter when there won't be any food. We can learn lessons from the squirrels and other animals," Mama said.

Mama was always so practical. I liked to take every day as it came and not worry about tomorrow. I was not sure that the squirrels really knew how to store food, but that was what Mama said, so I believed it was true.

I had to admit that the garden looked beautiful when the plants started producing. There was nothing tastier than a garden tomato. Mama loved to walk in the garden at dusk when it was cool, and I followed her as she looked on the fruits of her labor.

Mama always had what she called the "company cupboard" where she stored her canned fruits and vegetables. She also canned meat which came in handy if company dropped in unexpectedly. That happened quite regularly.

One day I was standing on the front porch trying to dress my kitty, Tiger, in one of my doll dresses, when suddenly someone pulled into our driveway. I dropped the kitty, and she went scampering off with the dress flying in the breeze.

"Mama, Mama," I called excitedly, "we have company!"

"Hold your horses, Mary Ellen," she said. "Don't act like you've never seen another person in your life."

I wasn't sure what she meant by that, but I ran out to the yard to see who had come to visit.

To my surprise, it was my Aunt Ellen and her boys. The two older boys, Victor and Harry, were close to my age, and little Jack was about six years younger than me. They lived on a farm near Sioux Falls and didn't come to visit too often.

"Victor, Harry!" I called as they got out of their car. I ran to meet them and tried to give them hugs, but they really didn't like to get hugs from girls.

Mama came out to greet them and said, "John should be home for dinner in about an hour. Can you stay and eat with us?"

Even though Aunt Ellen hesitated, her boys jumped up and down crying, "Can we, Mama? Can we stay?"

"Well, we have come quite a way, so I guess we should stay and visit some," Aunt Ellen said.

That was all we kids had to hear and we were off like a shot to the grove to see what treasures we might find, with Mama yelling after us, "Stay within ear shot so you can hear when I call for dinner!"

Little Jack had to stay with his Mama and go into the house. Edith got the duty of watching him so Mama and Aunt Ellen could visit.

I know we would have something wonderful for dinner that day, as Mama always had plenty in the "company cupboard." She could whip up a cake "before you could say Jack Russel," as Papa always said.

We were busy climbing trees and playing cops and robbers when we heard the call to dinner. We knew not to dilly-dally around but go straight to the house and get washed up, as we had gotten pretty dirty playing in the grove.

Just like that, instead of having only four mouths to feed, we had eight. I started to see Mama's wisdom in having a big garden.

We sat around the table for a long time after the meal. I was happy about that because I could put off doing the dishes. Mama and Aunt Ellen told stories about things they remembered from the past. We kids loved hearing about the "olden days" as we always called them. Papa joined in for a while, but soon he had to get back to work.

Suddenly, Aunt Ellen said, "Well boys, we better get on the trail home so we will be there in time for chores."

They begged to stay longer, but Aunt Ellen won out and soon they were piled in their car and driving out our driveway. Mama, Edith, and I stood on the front porch and waved to them as they drove out of the yard.

"Well, I guess we better get the dishes done now," Mama said.

"I'll help after I go to the outhouse, Mama. I really have to go," I said.

"Okay, but don't dilly-dally around and make Edith do them herself," Mama told me.

"I won't," I called back as I ran to the outhouse behind the milk house. I knew if I took too much time, Edith would finish up the dishes. She couldn't stand to let the dishes sit in the drainer. So, as expected, when I finally came back to the house, all the dishes were washed, dried, and put back in the cupboard. Mama was lying down for a nap, and Edith was working on some embroidery.

I liked to watch Mama and Edith sew, and sometimes Mama would thread a big needle and show me how to make nice even stiches. "See," Mama would say, "if you keep the stiches nice and even, it looks much better. Remember to take your time. A stitch in time saves nine." I wondered what that meant but soon I found out when all my thread balled up. My needle went in from the front when it should have gone in from the back, and soon my piece looked awful. I lost interest. I would much rather be outside watching Papa feed the pigs or working in the yard.

There was one thing I loved to help Mama with and that was baking. She made the most wonderful pies, and Edith was good at it too. I liked to stand on a little stool and watch Mama roll out the crust.

"Here, Mary Ellen," she said, "you can have this piece of dough and make your own pie. Just roll it out flat and then we can bake it."

After much rolling and pounding and adding more flour, my dough felt like shoe leather, but Mama still encouraged me by saying, "That's great, Mary Ellen. You will have a tasty pie. Now sprinkle it with a little sugar and cinnamon and we'll put it in the oven with Edith's and my pies."

When Papa came in for supper he said, "My, what is that wonderful smell?'

"Papa," I said as I ran to him, "I made my own pie, and it was good!" I had, of course, eaten it as soon as it came out of the oven.

I think I liked baking because of all the time I spent making mud pies and cookies in my playhouse. It was a treat to make something real that I could actually eat.

More often than not, Mama said, "Run outside now and let Edith and I finish this up." I think she was just tired of having me jumping around and not really doing much.

I was more than willing to run free out into the world I loved. I had the kitties and our dog, Spot. I got that name from my first-grade reader. The dog in the book was named Spot, and I learned how to spell it. I loved trying to dress the kitties up in doll clothes and attempting to take them for a ride in the buggy down the driveway. Most of the time they rebelled, and I had to chase them to retrieve the doll clothes.

Spot was my best friend, and he would follow me all over the yard, but sometimes Papa needed him to help get the cows in from the field. He was a good cattle dog and kept them in line as they slowly walked to the barn.

Another of my favorite farm animals was the newborn baby pigs. I was able to get close enough to the babies to be able to hold one or two at a time. The Mama pigs knew me, as I would spend time rubbing their backs and scratching them. They didn't feel threatened by me and allowed me to hold their babies. I had named two of the Mama pigs, Black Foot One and Black Foot Two. Not very original, but they seemed to respond to their names.

Even though I loved being outside, when I came into the house coughing and sneezing, Mama would say, "Mary Ellen, you should not be outside so long. I think the weeds and things outside are causing your coughing and sneezing. You better stay inside the rest of the day and play in the house."

"Oh, Mama", I said, "I can't stay in the house all the time; it's just too boring." But Mama insisted and found things for me to do to keep busy. There were always floors to be swept, furniture to be dusted, and beds to be made.

I could tell when Mama was not feeling well. She would sit in her rocker and do needle work. She would hum tunes from church and seemed happy, but I could tell she was struggling to see her needle work. She loved sewing and doing embroidery, but her eyesight was worsening every year. She was one of the few people I saw wear glasses, and she wore them from the time I could first remember. She also had to lie down at least a couple of times a day to nap. Her legs were so swollen, that when I took my little finger and pushed it into her flesh, it left a deep indentation that stayed that way for a long time. She had trouble breathing when she was up and around. She would stop and lean on the counter, or on the rake if she was in the garden.

I knew when I saw the doctor pull into the yard that he was coming to see Mama. My throat felt tight and I wanted to cry, as I was afraid Mama might die. Papa always comforted me by saying, "Little Tyke, you don't need to worry about Mama. Let the doctor take care of her, and she will be back to normal in a few days."

But she never really got back to normal, and I saw the worry in Papa's eyes. She would rally and would once again be able to work in the garden and around the house.

I always envied other girls who had a mother that could run with them and play or swing them in the swing and not have to sit down because they were out of breath. In my world, Mama was sick most of the time and I knew she could not do the things other mothers did for their children. But I loved her so and she was a Mama that I could come to when I was feeling troubled and scared. She'd let me sit next to her and talked to me and let me know that things were going to get better. She seemed so wise, and many times she had a phrase she used that seemed to help my despair. If I told her I was worried about something that might happen in the future, she would say, "We will cross that bridge when we get there." I wasn't sure what bridge she was talking about, but as I got older, I found the wisdom in her words.

If I wasn't kind to Edith, she would say to me, "Mary Ellen, you can catch more flies with honey than vinegar." I soon learned what honey and vinegar were, and it was true. Edith and I got along better when I became sweeter.

One saying Mama used made me laugh. If the PTA ladies were rushing around getting the food together for our monthly meeting at school, she would later tell Papa, "They were running around like a bunch of chickens with their heads cut off." I would giggle, envisioning the chickens we had butchered and how they continued to run and flop around after their heads were cut off.

It was hard for me to feel close to my Mama, as I always thought she might not be with us one day. Whenever I thought about that, it would make me sad, so I didn't talk about the things I worried about. I didn't want Mama to feel sad and make Papa worry about me. In my nightly prayers, I asked God to make my Mama better, but I was beginning to think that it wasn't going to happen. It was hard having a Mama who was sick all the time, and I cried myself to sleep many nights thinking about it.

My Sister Edith

BEFORE I WAS BORN, my sister Edith was the only child and the only grandchild on both sides. She didn't have cousins to play with or much experience with other children her age. She was born the same year the Titanic sank, 1912. Soon after I was born, she started school.

She was a little girl in an adult world, and because of that, she had a hard time relating to children her own age. She was very smart and learned to read before she entered school at age six. In first grade, the teacher soon found that she could read the reader and primer, so she was moved to second grade. The school was closed a great part of that year, 1918, because of the Spanish flu epidemic.

Edith really didn't like going to school very much, as some of the older children would tease her and she would come home most days crying. Mama and Papa had both been teachers, so they began to teach her at home. She liked being home with them. When she returned to school, she was in the third grade and managed better.

She used to tell me about what it was like when she started school. She would rather stay in at recess and read when the other children would run outside to play.

"The teacher tried to make me to go outside and play," she told me one day, "but I just didn't want to. I was afraid that the big kids would tease me, so I stayed inside most recesses."

She liked staying inside with Mama and helping around the house. She would read day and night if Mama would let her. I loved when she would read me stories from her reader.

She was very good at needle work, and Mama would praise her for her tiny straight stitches. She hardly ever had to rip out a seam. Mama would make my doll clothes, and then Edith would put some embroidery around the neck and bottom of the dresses.

"Mama," I said one day while holding out one of my doll dresses, "I need a new dress for Matilda. This one got all dirty and torn."

"Why, Mary Ellen," Edith said with exasperation, "I worked so hard on that embroidery for you. What in the world happened to it? I suppose you were dressing the cats again, and it looks like they ran through a mud puddle!"

Mama said, "Mary Ellen, I'm not going to make new dresses for you to dress the cats and ruin them. From now on, you use the old dirty ones on the cats and save the new ones for your dolls. Do you understand?"

"Okay, Mama," I said as I hung my head, "I will try to be more careful with them."

Edith hardly ever got dirty unless she was helping with the hay in the field. When I was older, she and I would help Papa with the hay. She would stand on the haystack and move the hay around, and I would help Papa lead the horses pulling the hay rack. Papa, with his strong arms, would pitch the hay up on top of the stack. Edith was too afraid of the horses, but they liked me. Maybe because I always brought a piece of apple or carrot for them.

Edith was always very careful with her things, and she really didn't like me getting into them. I loved looking at her dresses hanging in the closet and admiring how nice they were all pressed and clean. She never got her good shoes dirty either.

Mama was always after me to be more careful with my good clothes and not to jump out of the swing with my Sunday dress on or get in the mud with my good shoes. Many times, I would forget what she said as I was having so much fun. Edith would tell me, "Mary Ellen, if you get your shoes dirty or tear your dress, Mama is going to give you a switching!" Somehow it was worth taking the chance. I don't think Edith ever got a switching in her whole life, at least not that I could remember.

When I started school, Edith was in eighth grade. I was quite small for my age, and she worried that the big kids would tease me.

"Mary Ellen," she said the day I was to go to school with her, "You stay close to me, you understand? I will make sure none of the big kids pick on you." I really didn't want to stay close to her, as then I couldn't run and play with the other kids. She would make me hold her hand, and after a while, I would squirm out of her hold and off I would go with her calling after me, "Mary Ellen, you be careful or you'll get hurt." She really did feel responsible for me, and I can't blame her for worrying about her little sister. After a while, she saw that I was able to take care of myself and would let me run and play, with her watchful eyes on me.

When I was old enough to play outside in my playhouse, Mama would have Edith come out and play with me, because Mama needed to take a nap, make bread, or just wanted me out of her hair for a while. Many times, Edith would bring a book along to sit and read. It wasn't much fun not having anyone to talk to about my baked goods, which I made out of mud from the nearby driveway.

Edith would much rather stay in the house all day, but one of our chores we shared was gathering cobs from the pig pen after the pigs had eaten the corn off of them. These were then burned in the cook stove in the kitchen. She never dared go into the pigpen to get the cobs, so I went in and threw them out of the pen. She would pick them up and put them in the basket we were to fill. Blackfoot One and Two just looked at me while I worked and grunted and went about their eating corn and rooting in the mud.

Edith thought when I was old enough that I could pick the eggs. That had been her job and she didn't like it one bit. The chickens would fly at her, and she would run out of the chicken house screaming and into the house. Then Mama would have to go out with her to pick the eggs.

One day when I was about five, Edith took me out with her to pick the eggs. I thought it was great fun and the chickens didn't bother me at all. They just looked at me with their beady eyes and clucked, then settled back down on their nest after I got their eggs. Soon I was able to pick the eggs myself and several of the hens became my pets. They would follow me all over the farm.

10

THE GOOD OL' SUMMERTIME

SUMMER COULD NOT COME soon enough for me. The last day of school seemed to drag on, but when the teacher finally told us to put our books away and stand to be dismissed for summer break, I was the first one on my feet.

I had been daydreaming all week about the things I would do this summer and had received a talking to from the teacher several times. I had also been caught whispering to Phyllis one time. The teacher gave me one of those evil-eye looks and I straightened up.

Soon the teacher rang the hand bell, which was the signal that we could file out of the school in an orderly manner. As soon as I hit the doorway, I let out a whoop, yelling "I'm free!"

"Mary Ellen," the teacher called back to me.

What did I do now? I thought.

"Mary Ellen, you forgot your lunch box," she said. "Go in and get it. You don't want to leave it all summer as it would smell pretty bad by next fall."

I ran in and quickly grabbed the only lunch pail that was left, and I was out the door again, running to catch up with Phyllis. She was my best friend, and we shared many secrets together.

"What did the teacher want?" she asked.

"Just to tell me not to forget my lunch pail, that's all," I said. "I was afraid she was going to ask me to stay after for whispering to you today and make me pound the erasers for her." Normally I liked cleaning the erasers, because I could make a real mess out on the steps, but today, I wanted to get going with summer.

"What are you going to do today?" Phyllis asked.

"Well…hmm. I don't really know, because I know Mama will have many jobs for me to do around the house since Edith won't be home for another week," I said. "Papa will be getting out in the fields soon and I'll need to help some with that. And I have to help clean the milk house. That's one job I hate! The spilled milk on the floor and around the separator is really stinky. I guess I'll try to lay low today so Mama won't have me in her hair and maybe get my playhouse set up."

"That sounds like a good idea," Phyllis said. "I'm going to help Mama make a cake today for my birthday on Sunday. Can you come?"

"Mama said I could, and I have a wonderful gift for you too. You will be surprised when you see it," I said.

As we walked along the dirt road, avoiding the puddles, we talked more about what we might do this summer. My birthday was coming up in July, and I was going to be ten. That made me feel so grown up to become a double number age. Usually for my birthday we asked Grandpa or Aunt Mary to come, but this year I was going to ask Mama if I could have a real party and ask some girls to come. I had it all planned.

We would play race, my favorite thing to do, as I was quite a fast runner even though I was still small for my age. Then we would play pin the tail on the donkey. I would ask Papa if he could make a donkey out of burlap, and we'd use tacks to pin the tail on it. We could play with my dolls, too, but I wondered if I was getting too old to play with dolls. *No, I don't think so,* I thought. Maybe when I get to be twelve or thirteen, then I should stop playing with dolls.

My favorite doll was Matilda. She had arms that moved and eyes that closed. Mama had made a beautiful dress and bonnet for her, and Edith added embroidery around the bottom. I was strictly told never to use that dress to dress up the cats.

Summer! Oh, so much to do. I loved climbing trees, for by now I was big enough to climb way up where the birds made their nests. Last winter the snow was so high I could walk on the snow and see the bird's nests that had been abandoned for the winter.

I loved setting my playhouse up. I asked Mama for all the old cans or kitchen items that were broken or no longer needed. I would put them in an old wooden peach crate I used for my cupboard, and out to the grove I went.

I first swept a spot clear of dead leaves with an old broom Mama let me have. Then I'd mark out where my walls would be using twine Papa gave me. I would then set my peach-crate cupboard up and place all my kitchen stuff in it. Sometimes Papa would nail it to a tree so it would be off the ground. My favorite imaginary sister, Betsy, would help me, and then we'd play house for hours.

I had a couple of little pans I would use to make mud pies, and I'd place leaves on top for a crust. I let them dry until the next day, and then I cut them in pieces. I had my imaginary friend, Jane, over for tea and crumpets. I didn't really know what crumpets were, but I thought it might be like pie. I spent many hours playing in my playhouse with my imaginary sister and friend. Sometimes I got so busy playing that I'd forget to come in the house when Mama called for supper. Then Papa was sent out to fetch me and tell me I needed to listen for Mama calling and not keep on playing.

"I will, Papa, I promise I'll listen for her to call from now on," I said. This scene was repeated many times during the summer, but Mama was usually pretty nice about it and didn't spank me.

One night at supper Papa said to Mama, "The Old Settlers Picnic is coming up in a couple weeks. Do you want to go, Mama?"

"I want to go," I said, even though he had not asked me. "Grandpa always takes me on the Ferris wheel and I love that ride. I'm not scared to be up so high, and Grandpa always sits by me and I feel very safe. Sometimes he leans way over and says, 'Who is that down there?' I squeal and act like I'm scared we'll fall out, and then he laughs and laughs. I love seeing all the people talking and all the buggies. They always have the best food too."

"Mary Ellen, you butted in when I was talking," Papa said sternly. "I was talking to Mama. Well, Ma, what do you think, should we go this year? It seems like there are fewer and fewer old settlers there every year."

"I think we should make an appearance. Like you said, many old settlers are gone now and the ones that are left really love it," Mama said. It is the highlight of the year. We definitely should go. Mary

Ellen, I don't mind you going on the Ferris wheel with Grandpa, but I don't want you to go by yourself."

"Oh, I wouldn't, Mama. I will only go if Grandpa goes with me…unless you want to go with me?"

"No, no, I don't like heights, but maybe Papa can go with you sometime. Now do you know what time it is, Mary Ellen?"

"It's time to clear the dishes and wash and wipe them. I will be glad when Edith gets out of school next week so she can help me," I said.

The next Sunday I went to Phyllis's birthday party, and she had a lovely and delicious cake. She also had party hats and balloons. I wondered if Mama would let me have party hats and balloons at my birthday. We played a game where everyone tied a balloon to their ankle, and we all tried to step on each other's balloon and break it. The person who was the last one with a balloon that had not been popped was the winner. I was pretty good at stepping on others' balloons and not getting mine popped, so I was the winner.

When it came time for Phyllis to open her gifts, I waited anxiously to see what she would say about my gift. It was a beautiful bracelet that Mama had helped me make with some blue and red beads from an old hat. It was on elastic string and could be slipped over your wrist. When she opened it, her eyes shone as she slipped the bracelet on. "Oh, thank you, Mary Ellen. I can't wait to wear it to school and show it to everyone."

We had so much fun, but soon it was time to walk home. I asked Mama that night if I could have a birthday party for my tenth birthday and have balloons and party hats.

"Maybe you can ask Phyllis to sleep over and we could have balloons for decoration, Maybe you can make your own party hats at the party. I will get some paper and some crayons for you to decorate them."

Mama was good at thinking up things like that, as she used to teach school and had a lot of ideas for parties. Papa agreed to make a donkey to play pin the tail on the donkey, even though there would only be the two of us. He said, "Maybe, Mama, Edith and I can play that game with you girls."

It was all set. Next time I saw Phyllis, I would invite her. It would be hard to wait, as my birthday wasn't until the twentieth of July, about a month away.

We all went to the Old Settlers Picnic, and I had a wonderful time riding on the Ferris wheel with Grandpa. Papa went with me once, but he wasn't as fun as Grandpa. Grandpa even took me to the drugstore to buy me an ice cream cone and we stopped at the popcorn stand to get popcorn.

Soon the day was over and we were headed home. I had a hard time staying awake as the car bumped and rumbled down our country road.

Papa said when we pulled into our driveway, "Mary Ellen, we're home now, wake up." But I was too tired to wake up, so Papa carried me into the house and tucked me into bed. That night I dreamed about the picnic and how much fun I had with Grandpa. I loved my Grandpa so much.

The other big event that happened every summer was the Sletten family picnic. Papa's aunts. uncles, brother, and sisters were all there. I got to see many cousins that I had not seen for a long time. We played on the playground equipment at the park where we met. Usually, it was in Sioux Falls or Beresford. They had wonderful playground equipment at those parks. I loved swinging on the huge swing sets, but I was too afraid to jump out of them as they were so much bigger than the ones at Pleasant Ridge School. The slide was twice the size of ours at school, and they both had merry-go-rounds which were the main attraction for the kids.

During the picnic, one of the older boys got all the little kids on the merry-go-round and started pushing it around and around, building speed as we all screamed with delight. Soon the inevitable happened. One of the little kids could not hold on anymore, flew off into the dirt, came up crying, and ran to their Mama. Then one of the Papas came over and stopped it, giving the boy a tongue lashing about going so fast. Of course, if we went on it after we ate our meal, there were always some who lost their lunch by the nearest tree. Then the rest of the day they spent lying on the picnic table. I never had that happen to me, and I was glad.

My birthday was approaching fast, and Mama had bought balloons at the store. She found some pretty paper in the closet that we could use for our hats. Papa made a fine donkey out of burlap. It looked just like the behind of a real donkey. The tail was made out of twine strings.

The day of my birthday Mama and Edith were busy in the kitchen making my cake and some delicious food for our supper. Phyllis was going to come about four o'clock so we could have time to play before supper. I helped Papa blow the balloons up but got dizzy and had to quit.

All was ready when Mama revealed the cake she had made. It was wonderful! Double layer with white, fluffy frosting in peaks on the top. She had sprinkled little silver balls on top that made it extra special. It had ten candles on it and I could hardly wait for supper to be over so we could eat it.

Soon Phyllis arrived and the party began. It was fun to watch Mama and Papa trying to pin the tail on the donkey. Papa was so tall, and the donkey had to be placed low enough for us to be able to pin the tail on, so he pinned the tail on the donkey's head! It was so funny! It was the highlight of the party, other than the delicious birthday cake.

That night Phyllis shared my bed and Edith slept in another room. We talked into the night about everything you could imagine. My tenth birthday was over and now I was double number age. I would never be single number age again.

Mary Ellen with sister, Edith. Mary Ellen is one.
Circa 1919

Mary Ellen with Uncle Charlie and Aunt Mary Nelson's dog, Sport
Circa 1926

AUNT MARY

Y AUNT MARY WAS a very central figure in my life. She came to help Mama for about a month after I was born. She bathed me every day on her lap and cared for Mama until she was strong enough to care for me by herself.

She was a schoolteacher and always asked to see my report cards whenever she visited.

"Why, Mary Ellen," she said, "you can do better than this in school. You just need to concentrate more on schoolwork and less on play. I expect to see more A's and B's on your next report card."

Even though she scolded me about my grades, she had a soft spot for me as she was a "free spirit" like I was. She loved to go to community events and was a member of many women's groups. She had been teaching school since she was seventeen and could tell you a thing or two about children.

Aunt Mary was my Papa's half-sister. They had the same mother, but her father died when she was only eight months old. My Grandma Sletten then married my Grandpa Sletten. She had an older brother, Peter, who died of diphtheria when she was two years old, and another older brother, Amil, who died after he was kicked by a cow when she was six years old. She didn't talk about them much but told us how she remembered when her brother, Amil, died. It was a very sad time, and it brought tears to her eyes when she talked about it.

She also talked about her half-brothers, Tom and Anthony, who both died young. Tom died in 1905 at the age of nineteen from the effects of having the measles. Anthony, or Tony as they called him, fought in the great war and was gassed in the trenches and died in 1919 at the age of twenty-three, before I turned one. Aunt Mary never talked about her brothers as half-brothers. They were her brothers and Grandpa Sletten her Papa.

I loved when Aunt Mary would tell the story about her family moving from Turner County, South Dakota, to Cedar County, Nebraska, in 1901. Grandpa Ingvold, Papa, Aunt Mary and Tom drove the cattle the one hundred miles south to Nebraska. They also had a wagon holding all their household belongings which Aunt Mary drove. Grandma Isabelle and the younger children took the train to their new home in Nebraska. It was hard for me to imagine my Grandpa, Papa and aunt Mary doing that

My Papa had the measles at the same time as Uncle Tom, and so did my Mama. Papa never had any aftereffects, but my Mama was left with poor eyesight and a weakened heart and kidneys. I don't know if Aunt Mary ever got the measles, but if she did, she was not affected as she was strong as a horse.

Aunt Mary could drive a team of horses with the best of them and traveled all around the state to different teacher's conventions. She loved to travel and had taken a long train tour with Papa and a group of teachers after they graduated from Wayne Normal School in 1909. She and Papa recounted that trip many times.

"John," Aunt Mary said, "remember we went to the Rocky Mountains and Denver, Colorado for that teacher's convention? I remember you could not get enough of the beautiful scenery out the train window, so you stuck your head out to get a better look. All of a sudden, you pulled your head back in and were moaning with your hand over your eye. Some ash from the train engine hit your eye, but I managed to get it out with my clean hankey. You thought you would be blind in that eye for the rest of the trip, but it was fine."

"My favorite part of the trip was climbing Pikes Peak," Papa said. "We were the only ones who completed the hike. All the other teachers started to run up the slope, because it was just a gentle hill. We met all of them coming down the mountain out of breath. They had not made it to the top because they didn't take it slow," Papa said. "Aunt Mary and I made it to the top, and we were the only ones on the trip who saw the splendid view from up there."

"Where did you go from there?" I asked.

Papa continued the story, "From Colorado, we went to Yellowstone, where we saw Old Faithful, then on to Salt Lake City, the Redwood Forests in California, and then up to Washington State and back to South Dakota. Yes, it was the trip of a lifetime for sure."

Aunt Mary added, "I liked riding on the trolly in Spokane. Those steep streets were something!" She got out her photo album and showed me the pictures she took on that trip, which included a picture of the group of teachers on the trolley.

I had a hard time envisioning my Papa going on such a trip, but I guessed that was back in the olden times when he was a young man.

Aunt Mary got married when I was seven, she was forty-four and I remember it well. Many people thought she would be an "Old Maid" and never get married, but she met Uncle Charlie Nelson at a church function. They courted for quite a few years before they got married. They lived on Charlie's farm by Hudson, South Dakota, and we visited them often.

The summer after they got married, Aunt Mary asked if I wanted to come and stay with her and Uncle Charlie. I piped up right away with "Yes!" So it was that Papa and Mama took me to Aunt Mary and Uncle Charlie Nelson's farm.

I had a lot of fun as long as Mama and Papa were there, but that evening, when Mama and Papa were driving out of the yard and down the road, I began to feel something in my tummy. I was trying to hold back tears, but suddenly I could hold them back no more. "I want to go home now," I sobbed, as Aunt Mary was tucking me into a very high bed with soft covers on it.

"Oh, you will be fine, Mary Ellen," Aunt Mary said. "I am here. You don't need to be afraid."

But I was not convinced and continued to cry that I wanted to go home. Finally, Uncle Charlie came to see what the commotion was and said to Aunt Mary, "If she wants to go home, we shouldn't make her stay. I'll get the car out and we'll drive her home."

So, home I went. When Papa and Mama saw us driving into their yard, they knew what had happened and said nothing about it. Mama took me and my suitcase upstairs, and as she was tucking me in, she said softly, "Mary Ellen, maybe when you get a little older you can stay with Aunt Mary again. You're just a little too young to be away from Mama and Papa."

Aunt Mary did ask me to stay with them again the next summer, and I was excited to stay with her and Uncle Charlie. Things went better this time. I was to stay for a week, but on the third day, Aunt Mary was busy in the kitchen, and I guess I was getting under foot when she suddenly said, "Mary Ellen, run outside now and let the wind blow the stink off of you."

I didn't think I was stinky, but I loved playing in the chicken coop as the chickens were like pets to me. After playing and naming half the chickens, I suddenly thought it would be fun to climb up to the rafters where the chickens roosted and see what it looked like up there. It was a great adventure to be roosting with the chickens. When I heard Aunt Mary calling me, I knew better than to ignore her call, so I climbed back down and ran to the house.

"Mary Ellen, what have you been doing?" she asked as she was standing at the kitchen sink with her back to me washing dishes.

"Oh, just looking at the chickens," I said as I scratched my head. "I climbed up in the rafters to see what the chickens see when they are roosting." I continued to scratch my head and then my arms and legs. Aunt Mary turned around and took one look at me scratching and she knew right away what was wrong. She said, "Why, Mary Ellen, Ishdaa! You have chicken mites all over you! Run to the granary and wait for me there."

The granary was a big building where they stored grain after the harvest, but now it was empty, and I waited there scratching and wondering what Aunt Mary was going to do to me for punishment. Soon I saw her coming across the yard with a big bucket and a towel and soap. When she got to the granary, she took off my clothes and

Aunt Mary Nelson with her team of horses.
Date unknown

put them in a gunny sack she had brought with her. Then she went about scrubbing me from head to toe with soap that burned my eyes. She didn't stop until she knew she had gotten all the mites off me. Then she put my clothes in the bucket of water and wrapped me up in the towel and took me to the house. After I was all dressed and the clothes with mites had been soaked with strong soap and hung out to dry, she gave me some dinner and said to Uncle Charlie, "I think it best if Mary Ellen not stay so long. She just has to be watched every minute and I am too busy for that!" So, after dinner we loaded up in their car and back home I was taken. Papa had to laugh when he heard the predicament I had gotten into. Mama sent me right to bed for a nap, which was good, as I was really tired after the day's events.

The next year I was nine and old enough to attend a day camp, which was held in Hudson. I loved it as I got to meet many new friends and we could swim and play softball. Aunt Mary took me there in the morning and picked me up in the afternoon. It lasted two weeks, so it helped Aunt Mary out as she didn't have to figure out what to do with me every day. When camp was over, I stayed another week and loved playing with Uncle Charlie's dog. He knew all kinds of tricks like roll over, sit, play dead, shake hands, and beg. I could give him commands and he would obey. My dog never learned any of that.

Aunt Mary was very good at keeping me busy and she didn't make me nap, which I liked. She had a lot of old dresses and fancy hats in her closet and let me play "dress up." I put on one of the dresses, which was much too long for me, and one of the hats. She also had long white gloves that covered my whole arm. Then I pranced out to the living room and pretended that I was a movie star. Uncle Charlie whistled and clapped for me as I made my turns.

Aunt Mary was a great cook and told me, "Mary Ellen, I was making meals for our family when I was your age." She could make the best cake. She was very patient with me and when it was time to go home, I was sad, even though I was a little homesick. She had such interesting stories about "the olden days" when she and Papa were children on the Dakota prairie. She had countless stories about her many travels. I was never bored at Aunt Mary's house.

For the next few years, I stayed at Aunt Mary's and went to summer camp. When I got bigger, I was expected to stay home and help with the fieldwork, which wasn't so bad. Papa made it fun, and Uncle Sam came and helped too. Before long it was time to go back to school. I had a lot of fun in the summer and would tell the teacher all about my adventures at Aunt Mary's house.

RHEUMATIC FEVER

THE CHRISTMAS AFTER I turned ten was memorable. We put on a school play, and I got to recite a "piece" as they called it.

I decided to do Robert Louis Stevenson's poem, "The Swing." I had practiced until I nearly drove my mother to distraction. I worked on getting the inflection in my voice to go up and down when I said "up in the swing and down again." I also used my arms to show the motion of the swing.

Soon it was my turn to say my piece. I stood tall and straight as I began.

"The Swing" by Robert Louis Stevenson[1]

---

1 Stevenson, Robert L. (1916). "The Swing." Public domain: https://poets.org/poem/swing

How do you like to go up in a swing,
Up in the air so blue?
Oh, I do think it the pleasantest thing
Ever a child can do!

Up in the air and over the wall,
Till I can see so wide,
Rivers and trees and cattle and all
Over the countryside—

Till I look down on the garden green,
Down on the roof so brown—
Up in the air I go flying again,
Up in the air and down!

I really related to this poem as swinging up high was one of my favorite pastimes at school. I often wished that I could fly like the birds so I could look over the land from high above. Sometimes I dreamt that I could fly, and just when I was soaring high above the farm, I would wake up. I was always disappointed that it was just a dream.

The Christmas program also consisted of many songs, one of which I really enjoyed and sang out quite loud was "Frosty the Snow Man." Papa had determined that I could not carry a tune as one time he sat me down by the piano and hit a note, then said, "Mary Ellen, sing this note."

What came out of my mouth was far from that note, or any note really. Papa exclaimed, "Hopeless monotone!" But I was not deterred from singing and lustily sang out in school and church.

My favorite song in church was "Up from the Gravy He Arose." I didn't learn until much later that it was "Up from the Grave He Arose." Papa got used to my singing off key and smiled as I sang out the hymns.

The Christmas program for church was much different from our school program. We acted out the story of Mary, Joseph, and Baby Jesus. I never did get to play Mary, but I was satisfied at being an angel with beautiful wings who stood over the manger where baby Jesus slept. I sang out "Away in the Manger" at the top of my lungs, which brought some chuckles and smiles from the crowd. I loved being the center of attention, and even though I didn't get the main role, I beamed with joy at the reaction I was receiving.

After the program was over and we were filing out of the church, we were given brown paper bags that contained an apple, an orange, some unshelled peanuts, and some ribbon candy. The ribbon candy was my favorite as it was the colors of Christmas—red, green, and white. Mama used to make brown sugar candy, which was my favorite too, but it wasn't as pretty as the ribbon candy.

When we got home, Mama and Papa brought out the presents and set them on the table where the small tree stood. We usually had one present each, but it was the most exciting thing I could think of. One year I made a black potholder and sewed a cat on it for Aunt Mary. This year I had a big present, but it was not on the table. It was sitting up against the wall in the dining room. I guessed what it was before I even opened it but didn't let on. When I opened it, I screamed, "A sled!" Grandpa Sletten had made it for me. I could hardly wait for tomorrow to try it out.

The next day Papa and I went out in search of a hill that would be high enough to slide down. The land around our farm was mostly flat, but Papa managed to find a small hill by the creek bank and sent me down. I whooped all the way down and begged him, "Again, again!" When I had gone down the hill enough times to satisfy myself, Papa pulled me back to the house. That was a wonderful Christmas, one I would always remember.

School was out, so I was free to play outside in the snow. When I came in with my rosy cheeks and fingers and toes half frozen, I sat by the fire while Mama made me some hot chocolate milk. I felt so warm and cozy there in the kitchen by the stove.

One day about a week after Christmas, I awoke with a terrible headache and my arms and legs ached. "Mama, Mama," I called. Soon she was there feeling my head and looking at every inch of my body. "Mary Ellen, you just stay in bed, and I'll bring you something for breakfast after I call the doctor to see if he can come out and take a look at you."

I didn't want the doctor to come as that usually meant having to take some nasty tasting medicine, but I was feeling so bad that I was glad to hear that the doctor would be coming out to see me later that day.

I have never hurt so much in all my life. My legs, arms, back, and head pounded with pain. I could hardly move my legs, and my arms hurt just to put them up to my face to eat. When I had to use the chamber pot, I could hardly stand and sit. I was never so glad when I was done and could return to my bed. I shook all over uncontrollably and no number of blankets could keep me warm. Then I got terribly hot and broke out in a cold sweat. Mama had to change my sheets several times a day.

Finally, Dr. Parks arrived and poked and prodded, took my temperature, and looked me over from head to toe. He looked solemnly at Mama and Papa and said, "I'm pretty sure she has rheumatic fever. This can follow a sore throat and then goes into a full body effect. It can be very dangerous and have lasting consequences for years to come. I will give you something to help with the joint pain and the fever, but besides that, there is nothing more I can do. I will stop out and see her every five days or so to see how she is getting along. Be sure to have her drink plenty of water and try to keep her cool so her temperature does not rise too high. You might want to move her to a room on the main floor, as you will be kept busy back and forth."

When Dr. Parks left, Papa carried me downstairs to a small cot we had in the living room and lay me down on it. I felt better at once knowing they were close at hand. "You can stay here until you're feeling better. Mama and I will be close by in our room," Papa said. "You can call whenever you need anything, and we will be at your side. Now go to sleep and let the medicine that Dr. Parks gave you work." I was soon fast asleep, dreaming that I was flying far above the earth.

I was bed-bound for about three weeks. I only got up to use the pot and went right back to the cot. Aunt Mary came and helped take care of me until she had to go back to school after Christmas vacation. Edith was home, but was told not to come in contact with me for fear she might contract rheumatic fever.

I was so weak, I had to have Mama or Papa hold me up when I used the pot. I didn't feel like eating as my head ached too much and my arms hurt to raise my spoon to my mouth, so Mama tenderly fed me and helped me drink. I slept most of the time, which helped Mama get some rest herself. Sometimes I thought how worn out she looked and worried that she might get what I had, but the doctor told them it usually affects young children between the ages of six and fourteen. He told them I could be in bed for weeks, and after would need to basically learn to walk again, as my muscles would be so wasted and weak. I learned later that he also told them it could weaken my heart. I heard Mama and Papa talking in low tones in the other room.

"John," Mama started, "I just never thought Mary Ellen would get this sick. She is always so strong and rambunctious. I will never complain again of her running through the house and dragging in dirt from outside." Then she began to cry softly.

"Mama, don't worry, we will get through this," Papa said. "God will keep Mary Ellen safe and help her regain her former active self. We have prayed over her many times, and that is all we can do, besides what the doctor instructed us. She's a fighter. Remember when she had her tonsils out and how she fought the doctor and me? We could hardly hold her down." Tears were filling Papa's eyes as he looked in upon his Little Tyke.

Gradually I started to feel better and was able to sit up and eat by myself. I still had to have someone help me use the pot, but that also got better. The doctor was right. I did have to learn how to walk all over again. Mama usually helped me take the first steps across the floor. I tired easily and had to lie down after only a few steps. Each day Mama helped me take more steps and then moved my legs and arms around while I lay on the cot. Finally, I was able to sit up in a soft chair and look out the window. I sat in the dining room by the big window with small squares of stained glass at the top. I loved sitting there in the sun with the colors spreading across the dining room floor.

By mid-February, I was strong enough to return to school. I was never so happy to go back to school and see all my friends! By the time spring came, I was outside running and playing like I had the year before. Mama was true to her word and never again got upset with me for running in the house or bringing dirt in from my playhouse. She just took a deep breath and looked the other way.

Edith Goes to College
1929

Edith was going off to college at Eastern State Teachers College in Madison, South Dakota. Life was a flurry of activity at our house. Mama was making some new dresses for Edith, even though she was not well most of the time. Edith shopped for the needed supplies, and they were carefully packed in the old trunk.

The year was 1929, and times were hard. There was a drought, and crops were very scarce or none at all. Papa managed to have enough money for Edith to enter school, and she worked to help with the rest of the expenses.

I was used to Edith going to stay in town while she was in high school, but now she would be much farther away. She could only come home at Christmas. I missed her. We had grown closer as I got older. We worked together tending the garden, feeding the animals, working with Papa in the field, and I had even begun to enjoy our time together while doing dishes in our comfortable kitchen.

"Edith," I said one Sunday as we were in the kitchen cleaning up from our Sunday dinner. "I know you will have to do a lot of studying at school, but I hope you will have some fun too. It seems to me that you are always so serious and don't have much fun."

Edith slowly answered me. "Mary Ellen, having fun is not the most important part of life. We have to study hard, work hard, and make our way in this world," she said. "I wouldn't have gotten the good grades I did in high school if I hadn't studied hard and missed some of the parties that were going on. I look at Papa and Mama and see how they were able to get their education by working and studying hard. Even though they are not using that education now, they always have that to fall back on if times get hard."

I was not so sure what she said was right, because I always thought of the saying, 'All work and no play makes Jack a dull boy.' I was starting to realize, however, that I needed to buckle down and try to get better grades. She got accepted to college because of her grades in high school, and I wanted to go to college also.

I was going into fifth grade, and Mama had instructed me to buckle down and not to bring home anything less than B's on my report card. That was quite a high expectation for me, but I dutifully told her that I would try my hardest.

Soon the day came to take Edith to college, and early in the morning we were all loaded into our car for the long journey. It was about seventy miles from our farm, and it would take us about three hours to get there. Then we had to unload all of Edith's things and get her settled in her dorm room. I was so excited to see a real college where Edith would spend the next two years.

Mama had some tears in her eyes as we were pulling out of the college campus. Papa patted her on the hand and said, "Now, now, Nellie, this should be a happy time. Edith is taking that first step into adulthood. I know we will all miss her, but we must realize that she can't stay at home forever. We wouldn't want that for her. She needs to test her wings and fly."

"I know," Mama said through her tears." "I can't believe that she is all grown up. It just seems like yesterday when she was born. She was so tiny that we didn't know if she would live. I guess I'm being a little selfish. She is such a help to me around the house."

I piped up. "Mama, I am big enough to help with everything around the house like Edith did. I know I can be just as much help to you as she was."

"Mary Ellen," Mama replied, "I know you are getting so big and have become a wonderful help to me when I'm not feeling well. I'm sure I will cry when you go off to college someday too."

During the long ride home, I thought about what I wanted to do when I was ready to go to college. I had never thought about that before, so I thought about all the possibilities. Maybe I could be a nurse, but then I thought about how Mama and Papa discouraged Edith from that profession, because "nice" girls didn't become nurses. I wasn't sure what that meant, but I knew Mama and Papa were against it. I could be a secretary at the bank; that would be interesting. Or maybe I could work in the office at the college and have a nice typewriter that I could click away on. That looked really fun! I had been impressed with the speed with which the lady at the college office typed out the form for Papa to sign. That really intrigued me.

So, if I couldn't be a nurse, maybe I could be a secretary and learn to type like the lady in the college office. She wore high heels that clicked on the floor when she walked across the room, and she had on a lovely dress and beautiful red lipstick. *Someday I want to wear high heels that click on the floor and red lipstick just like her,* I thought.

Soon we were back home and there were chores to be done. I really missed Edith that night as I had to help Papa and Mama finish the chores and then help Mama fix something for supper. I also cleaned up all the dishes, because Mama was very tired from the long day and went to bed early.

Later that evening, Papa and I were alone after all the dishes were done, and we were sitting in the living room while Papa was reading the paper. I thought it was a good time to see what he thought about my desire to be a secretary.

"Papa," I asked timidly, "do you think I could be a secretary some day? I really liked the lady at the college office who typed up the papers you needed to sign. I think that would be fun to do, and I liked her high heels too."

"Well, Mary Ellen, being a secretary is an important job, but I know it means that you sit in an office all day at the typewriter," Papa said. "You have to be able to type very fast to get a good job. Plus, I am sure the college ladies' feet hurt every night when she goes home. Do you think you could be confined to an office all day?" Papa asked.

"It would be hard for me, but I think if I really enjoyed it, I would be okay," I said. "I could sit by a window and look out from time to time."

"Well, Mary Ellen, you still have to get good grades to get into a college," he said. "Maybe when you go to high school you can take some typing classes and see if you really like it or not. For now, you better get off to bed as you start school tomorrow. "

School tomorrow—the summer had gone by so fast! I was happy to see my friends every day, but not excited about trying to get better grades. I was determined to do better as I only had four more years in grade school, and then I would be going to high school.

That night I dreamt I was a secretary and wore high heels that clicked on the floor and red lipstick.

At Christmas time, Edith took the train to Canton, and we went to pick her up. I was happy to see her, but she seemed changed somehow. She was more grown-up and was more fun too. She told me about what she had been doing at college and the friends she had met. She even had met a boy that she really liked. His name was Jack, and she talked about things they had done together, like taking long walks across campus and studying together in the library.

Wow, I thought, *Edith has a boyfriend?* She didn't mention him to Mama or Papa, as she thought they would think she was too young to have a boyfriend, but she pointed out that Mama was Papa's girlfriend at the same age.

That Christmas was a happy time with our little family back together. Mama was not doing well, however. She had to spend much of the time in bed, and I was glad that Edith was home to help with the housework.

One Sunday after dinner, Papa was looking out the west window and noticed something outside that was curious to him.

"What in the world?" he said. "What are those men doing running from our haystack?" He called the sheriff who came out to inspect the situation. What they found were shoe tracks around the back side of our haystack. Papa noticed that the back side was disturbed, so the sheriff dug into the stack and found something very interesting.

"It seems that someone has been using your haystack to hide some of their "bootlegging" activity. I guess they thought that your field would be the last place the law would look for liquor," he said with a laugh.

But the laugh was on the bootleggers, because they left tracks in the snow which led the sheriff directly to their house. We all had a good laugh when Mama got up from her nap. Papa and Mama were very much against drinking alcohol and were in favor of prohibition. From then on, Papa kept a close eye on his haystacks.

Soon we were taking Edith to the train in Canton, and she waved to us from the train window. I had a sad feeling seeing her train pull out. I thought to myself, *Our childhood as we know it is almost gone.*

*Mary Ellen (right) with sister Edith (left) at
Edith's high school graduation. Circa 1929*

THE DIRTY THIRTIES

Times were hard everywhere in the 1930s, but our family did not suffer like some who lived in other parts of South Dakota. We always had food on the table because Mama preserved her garden produce. We carried water from the well to water the garden, or collected what little rain was caught in the rain barrels under the down spouts. There was no rain for months at a time. Mama sewed clothes for us to wear out of flour sacks. We didn't mind wearing them because everyone else was doing the same thing. There were no crops for most years, except 1936, when we had a very small crop.

The egg prices were so low it didn't pay to take them into town, so we ate a lot of eggs in every form possible. One time Papa took a load of hogs to Sioux Falls but brought them home because there wasn't a market for them.

There was a layer of dust on everything. When we got to school and opened our dinner pails, they were full of dust. Many times, we were unable to eat our lunch due to the dust. Mama stuffed rags under the doors and windowsills to try to keep the dust out, but it didn't help much. We had to wipe the table off before we ate, and we turned the plates and cups upside-down to keep them free of dust, but by the time we sat down to eat, everything was covered in dust.

"I hate this dust," I said one day as I wiped the table off for what seemed like the hundredth time. "How long will this last, Papa? I don't know if we can live like this for much longer."

"Mary Ellen, we have to trust that the Lord will help us through and give us our daily bread like the Bible says. Never doubt God and what he is able to do. All the trials we go through develop our character, with the help of God." he answered.

I knew that was the truth, but I hated all the dust, and I knew Mama was weary trying to keep up with all the dust in the house. Because Edith was away at college, it was my job to help Mama with the housework.

The hot wind blew for days on end, and dirt piled up like snowbanks around the farm. It filled the ditches along the roads. When the wind finally stopped and I went out to play, it was like being on another planet. Everywhere was only dirt, no grass or even weeds. Some of the dirt was red, and I wondered why that was. I had never seen any red dirt in the fields of Canton after Papa plowed. I asked Papa about the red dirt, and he said, "It must be from Redfield, South Dakota." I had never been to Redfield, but I envisioned the crimson landscape and how strange it must be there. Papa told me how farmers in that part of the state were really in dire need and having to go to food lines just to feed their families.

Dirt drifted around buildings and in the trees, which were mostly dormant. I liked playing on the hardened drifts of dirt as if they were snow. Papa and I had to go out to feed the animals, even though the wind sent dirt in the air, and we could hardly see our way. When we got to the barn, our mouths and noses were full of dirt, and we had to blink our eyes to get the dirt out of them. We sold most of our cows but kept a few milk cows. Papa managed to harvest enough hay to feed the cows we kept. When the first snow fell in the winter, it came down brown and didn't look like the same glistening white that I loved.

What the drought didn't take, the onslaught of grasshoppers did. They filled the air with a noise I had never heard before, and one I hoped never to hear again. It was a loud buzzing, cracking roar. It was deafening at times.

Mama said one afternoon when the grasshoppers were descending, "Mary Ellen, run out and get the clothes off the clothesline before the grasshoppers eat all our laundry." I reluctantly ran out, and amid their flying wings and clinging legs, I pulled the clothes off the line. They had already started chewing holes in things. They ate anything—including the clothes pins and the clothesline, any blade of grass in the fields, and even the fence posts were not left untouched. The chickens were busy eating up the grasshoppers, so they were well fed. We ate a lot of chicken.

"Mama, do we have to have chicken, chicken, and more chicken all the time?" I complained one day. "I don't think I can eat another chicken in my whole life."

"These chickens are keeping us alive," Mama said. "Don't complain, Mary Ellen. If you don't want to eat it, that leaves more for the rest of us. God has blessed us with the food we have. There are many who are starving during this drought. We need to be thankful," she said. "This too shall pass."

When Edith graduated from college, she came home for the summer, and I was so happy to have her home. She told me all about school and how she graduated in the top ten percent of her class. I was proud of her and hoped I could follow in her footsteps.

She got a teaching job for grades first through eighth at a country school in Turner County in the fall of 1931. She was hoping to get a job teaching eighth-grade math but couldn't find any of those positions. She taught for one year and things seemed to be going well. But the second year, after the first semester, Edith came home crying.

"Oh, Mama," she cried, "I am so unhappy. I just can't deal with the older boys. They won't listen and do what I tell them. The last straw was when they lifted me up and sat me on top of the piano. All the children were laughing and pointing at me. All I could do was cry. It brought back memories of when I started school at Pleasant Ridge. The children teased me unmercifully, and the big boys carried me out into the field and left me there to find my own way back."

"Edith," Mama said as she put her arm around her. "We love you just for who you are. You have always been sensitive about things, and that's all right. Don't worry, Edith, you will find your niche in life and flourish in it."

"I know, Mama, I just feel like I let you and Papa down after you helped me so much to go to college. How can I ever pay you back for what you have done?" Edith sobbed.

She told me later that night through tears, "I'm afraid I'll be an old maid, Mary Ellen. Jack wrote to me and told me he has another girl, and they are getting married this summer." Edith was twenty and I was fourteen and in the eighth grade.

I tried to comfort her. "Oh, Edith, you will find someone else and get married and have a bunch of kids; I just know it." I don't know if I made her feel better, as later in the night I awoke to her sobbing in her bed. I didn't know what to do to help, but I tried to be kinder to her from then on.

Edith continued to stay at home, and I was glad for the help, as Mama had a lot of bad days and spent much of the time in bed. Edith took care of Mama just like a nurse would. She would help her bathe and get dressed each day. It was hard to see Mama needing so much help with things that she could always do herself before. I kept praying that God would make her better, even though I wasn't sure that was going to happen.

In 1931, I was in eighth grade, and I enjoyed my last year at Pleasant Ridge. My grade school years were some of my happiest, with a lot of fond memories. I had a good friend, Elna Nelson. She and her little brother, Robert, walked with me to and from school every day.

One day in November, we cut across the Hicks' pasture on our way to school. All of a sudden, we noticed the cattle standing not too far from us, and I said, "Elna, we have to run so the cows don't get us!"

We all took off with our legs and arms flying. Little Robert managed to keep up. When we came to a woven wire fence, we scrambled over it. Elna managed to get over it and helped her little brother to the other side. When I climbed over, I caught my long brown stocking on the top wire, which was barbed, and tore a big hole in it.

"Oh no, Mama will be upset with me for tearing my stockings," I said. "I think she'll be able to mend it though. Maybe I will ask Edith to fix it, and Mama will never have to know."

When we got to school, it was much like other days, but the sky was overcast and the wind was howling outside our warm school room. I was studying my spelling words, writing each one ten times. As I worked, I fingered the hole in my stocking, making it even bigger. I could feel the grit of dirt under the paper on my desk. I noticed the teacher looking out the window many times and checking the oil in the lamps, which hung on the walls in between each window.

Suddenly, things grew darker and the wind fiercer. The teacher said, "Children, I'm going to dismiss early. It looks like blizzard weather. Don't be afraid; there's no snow, but go straight home."

As I put my spelling in my desk, I remembered Papa telling me about 1888 when many children were caught in a snowstorm and could not find their way home from school. It sent shivers down my spine. It was about half past three when we started for home. Elna was one year younger than me, and Robert was only eight years old. A fierce wind whipped the heavy door of the school out of my hands as we left the shelter of the schoolhouse. The sun was dimmed by all the dust flying around, and I could barely see the large silver maple trees by the ditch crossing. We headed west with the wind pushing our backs forward. It was fun running with the wind, and we were happy to be out of school early.

Soon we had to slow down, as the swirling dust and wind made walking harder and breathing almost impossible. Suddenly, I couldn't see anything. Even my own feet were lost in the swirling dust. I felt turned around and not sure which way to go. Robert fell in the road, and as Elna helped him up, she said, "Are we going the right way?" Robert stumbled again, and we found ourselves in the ditch covered with fine, powdery dirt.

"Mary Ellen," Elna questioned, "shouldn't we have come to the big cottonwood tree at the corner where the Hicks' farm is?"

As we started to climb out of the ditch, I saw a fence in front of us. I stumbled toward it and grabbed at the fence. My mitten caught the barbed wire on top of the fence, and I left it there.

By now, Robert was coughing and crying. "Tie your scarf around your face to keep the dirt out of your mouth," I instructed Elna as I helped Robert tie his scarf around his face. I pulled his hat down low on his forehead so all you could see were his scared eyes rimmed with dirt and tears.

I thought for a second, and then prayed, "God, please let me know which way we should go so we can get home safely." Suddenly, the wind let up slightly, and I looked at the fence with one strand of barbed wire on top. We had climbed over that fence this morning to get away from the cows, and now I knew we could follow the fence west and find our way home.

I managed to free my mitten and yelled to Elna. "I know we are going the right way! Just hang on to the fence and follow me!" It was hard for her to hear me, with the powerful wind and my voice muffled by the scarf over my mouth, but Elna took Robert's hand and they followed behind me, holding on tight to the fence.

The wind was colder now, and it was whipping us in the face. We stopped for a minute.

"Mary Ellen," Elna shouted, "we're going the wrong way, because the wind was at our backs, and now it is at our faces. We should have seen the large cottonwood tree by now."

"No, I know we are going in the right direction," I insisted. "I know we are going west."

"Well, just because you are fourteen doesn't mean you know everything," Elna shouted as she turned back. "I know we are going east, and I'm not going this way any further."

"Hang on to the fence," I instructed Robert as I grabbed Elna by the coat tail and pulled her back. "Remember this morning when we climbed over this fence to get away from the cows?"

"Yes," she replied, "but both sides of the road have fences on them."

"Yes," I shouted, "but the north side is a barbed wire fence, not a woven wire fence."

Elna answered, "You are right!"

Suddenly, I looked and could not see Robert anywhere. "Where is Robert"? I yelled at Elna. My heart stopped when I saw him huddled on the ground by the fence crying. "I fell down," he whimpered.

"Let's all rest a little here," Elna suggested as she tried to comfort little Robert.

"No!" I yelled. "We have to keep going! We will soon be at the Hicks'. If we stop, we may get so cold that we could fall asleep and never wake up."

I picked up Robert and tried to carry him as Elna followed behind. A sudden gust of wind hit us, and we all fell to the ground. Maybe it would be alright for us to rest just a few minutes, I thought. It was so hard to breathe, and I was so cold and tired. Robert was already asleep, and Elna was curled up against the fence with her eyes closed, shivering.

In a flash, I remembered how Papa had talked about the blizzard of 1888. He said, "You will always feel sleepy. Don't stop, or you will freeze to death."

I jumped up and shook Elna and Robert from their slumber. "Come on now, we have rested, and we need to keep going," I said.

We trudged on for what seemed like hours, holding on to the fence. That was our lifeline. Suddenly, I felt a tree in the fence line.

"Here is the first tree in the Hicks' grove!" I shouted. I started to cry for joy. Soon I saw the Nelson's old truck through the swirling, blinding dust as we entered the yard.

"It's Dad!" Elna shouted. "I saw Papa and Mr. Hicks in the back of the truck. Our fathers were coming to get us at the regular time that school got out, not knowing school had been let out early.

When we were brought into the warm farmhouse, we looked a sight! Our clothing was covered with dirt and our faces were black. The dirt had to be washed out of our eyes, and then we began to tell our stories to the adults.

Elna started. "We would've been half a mile east of the school and frozen stiff if it wasn't for Mary Ellen telling us which way to go."

"I was so scared," I said. "I prayed for God to help me know which way to go, and then I found the fence. I guess God answered my prayer."

Mrs. Hicks gave each of us a big mug of hot cocoa, and I thought about how God watches over us and answers our prayers, even when you are only fourteen.

READY FOR HIGH SCHOOL

THE SUMMER AFTER I graduated from eighth grade at Pleasant Ridge was fun and full of anticipation for starting high school in Canton. Since there was no bus service to town, children who lived in the country kept room and board in Canton, as my sister did. Papa and Mama had arranged for me to board with Mr. and Mrs. J. D. Hicks. My friend, Ethel Tuntland, was also going to be boarding there. We spent many hours planning the things that we would do when we "moved to town."

"Are you getting new clothes?" Ethel asked me one afternoon as we were sitting on our front porch.

"Well," I started, "I will have several dresses to wear that Mama has been busy sewing for me, but I worry if they will fit in with the other girls' clothes."

Lucy Keith was another friend that lived in Canton, and we had been friends for many years, as her family attended the same

Methodist church as us. She had gone to "town school" all her life and knew the ins and outs of what was proper to wear and how to act when you graduate to "town school." This was a big deal to me, as I thought country school was just fine, and then to learn that it may have been inferior to "town school" was quite a shock.

"Oh, Mary Ellen, I wouldn't worry about that," Ethel said. "If they're going to make fun of us because we went to country school, then we'll just turn our noses up and go the other way so we don't have to talk to them. That will make them feel bad that they didn't try to be friends with us. We'll have way more fun than they will anyway," Ethel said as she munched on the popcorn, we had made for ourselves.

"You're right, Ethel. I think I'm pretty good at thinking up lots of fun things we can do in town. We can walk downtown and pretend we're shopping for new dresses, even though we can't afford them. We can try on all different kinds of dresses and hats and then admire how beautiful we look in our expensive attire," I said as my mind was conjuring up more things we could do when we lived in town.

Ethel suddenly thought of something else. "Mary Ellen, I think it would be fun to go to the drugstore every day and get an ice cream cone or something."

Ethel liked to eat and especially liked sweets, something that I rarely got at home. I started thinking about going to the drugstore for ice cream every day. We sometimes stopped at the drugstore when Mama and Papa went to town to shop, but we didn't get to do that very often.

"Ethel, I will be so happy to be in town. It seems like here it's just dust, dust, and re-dust the house all the time. I know we'll be required to help Mrs. Hicks with her housework, and we'll have to keep our rooms neat and make our beds every day. But I think the dust won't be so bad in town. They have lots of trees and buildings to stop the wind from blowing the dust into the houses."

That summer was filled with helping Papa with the hay—one of the only crops that still grew—and helping around the house. Edith usually did most of the cooking since Mama was not well most of the time. She had gained some weight because of her inactivity, but she didn't have the stamina to keep up the housework and cooking for our family. She tried to help where she could but would soon have to sit or lie down for a rest. She would have good days and bad days, but bad days were more the norm.

One day she called me into the bedroom. "Mary Ellen, get the tape measure and measure my wrist, I think I'm losing weight."

I didn't think she had lost weight. In fact, I thought she was getting heavier. After finding the tape measure in her sewing basket, I measured her wrist. "Eight inches," I said, waiting for her response.

"That is much too big. I must lose weight, or I'll be big as an elephant soon," Mama replied with a little laugh. I thought it was an odd way to tell if you were gaining or losing weight. Most people used a scale, but we didn't have one of those, so I guess she thought if her wrist measurement went down that meant she was losing weight. I never thought Mama was especially careful about her weight before, but it seemed that she was obsessed with it now.

When I asked Papa about it later, he said, "Mary Ellen, your Mama is very sick and sometimes it affects her mind. I mean, sometimes she just doesn't think straight about things and worries about things that normally she would not worry about. The doctor told me last time he saw her that her kidney function wasn't good and that could affect her thinking. But we are not to worry, as he felt she has enough kidney function to live for many more years. He also said she may have had some small strokes, which could cause her memory and reasoning not to work like they should. We just need to reassure her that it doesn't matter if she gains a little weight, as eating is one of her only pleasures. I'm telling you this because you'll be in high school soon and you're old enough to understand this. We need to do all we can to help her enjoy what life she has left."

This shocked me, because no one had ever said that Mama was so ill she may not have much time left. Sure, she had to spend much of the day in bed, but there were times when she'd be better and would go along to church with us. But when we got home, she would spend the rest of the day in bed. I continued to pray that God would heal my Mama and help her be able to do all the things that she did as a young woman. I didn't want to believe that I wouldn't have her around for when I got married and had children.

That September Papa took me to town to the Hicks' house with my new clothes and got me settled in. I wished Mama could have come along, but she was just not up to it. Edith stayed home with her.

After I was settled, Papa and I went over to visit Grandpa. He was getting older and wasn't as spry as he once was. He loved to tell stories about when he was growing up.

"Why, it's my Little Tyke, my favorite grandchild!" he said as he greeted us at the front door. "What brings you to town today?"

"I'm moving into town and staying with the Hicks while I attend high school," I said proudly.

"I can't believe you're old enough to go to high school," Grandpa exclaimed. "Why, it seems like yesterday that your Grandma Sletten delivered you at the farm. That was quite a day for Grandma. It had been a long time since she delivered a baby, but she told me that it all came back to her. I miss her so much and think about when we'll be reunited in heaven someday."

There was a tear in Grandpa's eye, which he quickly wiped away with the handkerchief he kept in his pocket. He blew his nose noisily and put the handkerchief back in his pocket. Then we all sat down in the living room and visited for the rest of the afternoon. Grandpa offered to make us some French toast for supper before Papa had to head back to the farm. I loved Grandpa's French toast. He would put cinnamon in the eggs, and it was the best. Grandpa had been all alone in the house since Grandma passed away in 1921, almost fifteen years ago. It was hard for me to see Grandpa getting frail and walking with a cane. I always wanted to remember him as being energetic and able to keep up with Papa when he came to help in the field.

I guess that is part of growing up, realizing that you will not always have people you love with you forever. I knew the reality was I could be losing my mother and my grandfather sometime in the next few years, but I put that out of my mind and just enjoyed the time we had together now. Those memories will stay with me the rest of my life.

Starting High School

THE NEXT DAY ETHEL and I were up early and ready for school. We had our beds made and had used the indoor bathroom, which was a luxury for us, as we still used outhouses at home. I was feeling a little homesick as Papa usually took me to school the first day.

"Ethel, can you believe we are in high school?" I asked. "I am a little scared because the school is so big. What if I get lost and can't find my way to class?"

"Don't worry, Mary Ellen, Lucy will be there, and she knows her way around the school, because she's been there many times," Ethel said reassuringly.

"I'm sure after a few days I'll learn my way around," I said. "I'm glad we're in the same class so we can help each other. My Papa said there'd be about two-hundred kids in the school. That's more kids than I've ever seen in one place. Even at camp there were only about twenty-five kids, and I thought that was a lot!"

After a good breakfast, I put my school supplies and the lunch Mrs. Hicks made me in my new book bag. Mama had made it for me out of beautiful blue plaid, and it had a big button on the front which closed it. I had gotten new pencils, and Papa had given me an ink pen which had belonged to his brother Tom. I had seen some letters Uncle Tom had written, and he could write with such flair. He had mastered calligraphy letters, and I worked on doing that but had not mastered it. I wished that I could have met Uncle Tom and Uncle Tony, but they both died when they were young. Tom died before Mama and Papa were married from the effects of the measles. Tony died in the great war, after he was gassed in the trenches. I didn't ever know what that meant but knew many young men died in that war. Edith knew Uncle Tony, and she talked about him a lot, so I felt like I knew him.

"Okay, we better get going, Mary Ellen," Ethel said as she took the lead out onto the porch.

We had about three blocks to walk to school, but we were leaving in plenty of time. I felt so grown up as I walked along in my new dress carrying my book bag. What adventures awaited me in the next four years. I felt excited, but at the same time, I couldn't help but think about Mama, Papa, and Edith sitting around our table having breakfast and planning the day's work. I would be going home on the weekend, but that seemed a long way off right now.

"Here we are, Mary Ellen," said Ethel. "It sure looks like a huge building. I wonder how many other country kids will be here."

"I don't know, but when we have school achievement days, there are lots of other schools that take part. I wouldn't worry about it,

Lucy. I don't think we look like total hillbillies," I said, trying to be confident.

As we entered the school, the principal was there to greet us. "Well, Mary Ellen Sletten," he replied when I introduced myself. "I remember your sister, Edith. How is she doing?"

"Oh, she's fine," I replied. She's at home helping Papa and taking care of Mama.... Mama hasn't been well for some time."

I didn't want to get into everything right then, so I thanked him for asking, and Ethel and I moved down the hall to find our lockers. It was a sea of students going here and there. I could see many of the country kids that I'd seen before, but also many town kids that I didn't know. I felt like everyone was looking at us, but I guess they were looking at everyone. After we found our lockers, we walked slowly to our homeroom. I was more thankful than ever we were assigned to the same room. After we took our seats, the homeroom teacher gave each of us a map of where each classroom was located and instructed us on some of the rules we would have to follow. They didn't seem so hard.

1. No running in the hall.

2. You only have five minutes to get to your next class. If you come into class after the bell, you will have to stay in homeroom after school.

3. Treat everyone as you want to be treated. No pushing or shoving.

4. No bad language. (I didn't have to worry about that one. If I used any bad language, Papa would wash my mouth out with soap. I never had to have that treatment.)

5. No use of tobacco or alcohol on school grounds.

I looked at Ethel and raised my eyebrows. I couldn't believe that would be a problem, but I guess that's why they had to make the rule. There were many more rules, but these were the most important ones.

Soon the bell rang, and we were to go to our first classroom. Both Ethel and I were in the same English class and were easily able to find the room. As the teacher began, I thought to myself, *This is not so hard; I know everything she is teaching.*

By the last bell of the day, Ethel and I were happy the day was over. "My mind is so full, I don't know if it can hold much more," I said as we walked the three blocks to Mrs. Hicks' house. She asked how our first day of high school was, and we both told her what we thought of things. Then we went to our room and changed into our everyday clothes, as we had chores to do around the house. We carefully hung up our dresses so they would be nice for the next day.

That night as I lay in bed with Ethel sleeping soundly next to me, my mind again floated to the farm and what Mama, Papa, and Edith did that day. It was strange to be in a house without knowing that Papa and Mama were just downstairs if I needed them. I cried a little as I thought about them, but soon I was fast asleep.

The first week went by fast, and soon it was Friday and Papa came to pick me up. I was so happy to see him that I ran and gave him a big hug. "Papa, I've missed you so much all week, but I wasn't homesick—well, maybe just a little bit," I said.

After we stopped by the store to pick up some things Edith needed, we were headed down the road. It was good to be with Papa again as he wheeled the car onto the road. Our house was only ten miles from Canton, but it seemed like one-hundred miles that day. I didn't think we would ever get home.

After we turned onto our road, Papa stopped the car and said, "Mary Ellen, how would you like to drive?"

"Really?" I responded. "I don't know if I can do it."

But it didn't take me long to jump down from the passenger side and climb into the driver's seat. The seat had to be adjusted for my short legs, and Papa had to roll up a blanket so I could sit on it to see over the steering wheel.

After Papa gave me some instruction, I lurched ahead, then drove slowly down the road. Once I got going, it was so fun with the wind blowing in my face and the smell of fresh air. Papa kept an eye on things and had to grab the steering wheel a couple of times as I got too close to the ditch. I felt so grown up. He tested my ability to stop a few times, because, as he said, "Stopping is the most important part of driving."

When we came to the small grove of trees north of our house, Papa said he should drive into the yard as Mama would faint if she saw me driving. I stopped, and after we traded places, Papa drove into the yard. I didn't tell Edith about it, as she was too afraid to try to drive. She said, "I just get too nervous." I didn't know what there was to be nervous about.

Mama was sleeping when we got home, and Papa said not to wake her as she needed her sleep. Edith had a wonderful supper for us, and I was so happy being home with my family. I had many things to tell them about my first week of school.

Later when Mama got up, she seemed a little confused, but Papa said it was because she had been sleeping so hard. I didn't know about that, as some of the things she said just didn't make sense. I was worried about Mama and took the opportunity to talk to Papa later as we were in the barn doing the milking.

"Papa, how do you think Mama is doing these days?" I asked. "She seemed a little confused tonight, don't you think?"

"Yes, I've noticed that too, but I don't want to let on to her that anything is wrong. We had the doctor out earlier this week and he said her heart is very weak and her kidneys are not working like they should. Mary Ellen, I think you should prepare yourself that she may not be with us much longer."

I could hardly believe what I heard. "Oh, Papa, please don't say that! I know Dr. Park can pull her through. After all, didn't he save her when I was born? No one expected her to live through my birth, but she did, and now I'm sixteen and she's been with us all these years."

"Mary Ellen, the one thing your Mama wants is to see you graduate from high school. She said that is her last wish."

"Well, I know she will, and I know she'll see me get married, too. I just can't accept that she won't live to see my children."

"It is my prayer that you are right, Mary Ellen. Only the good Lord knows when our time has come. We have to trust that He knows what is best," Papa said.

That night as I lay in my familiar bed in my room, I prayed that Mama would gain strength and be able to be with us for many years to come. As I drifted off to sleep, my heart ached, and I had tears running onto my pillow.

17

SHENANIGANS AND FIRST LOVE

GOING TO HIGH SCHOOL was fun! I got to see my friends, Lucy and Ethel, every day, and we ate our lunches together outside in front of the school on the steps, unless it was raining or was too cold. Then we would eat in the school cafeteria with all the other students.

One day at lunch I asked them, "Girls, what do you know about Royle Johnson? He sits in front of me in study hall and he always turns around to say 'hi' to me. I think he is really the cat's pajamas." That was new slang I had learned since being in high school.

"He's in my English class and seems really nice," Lucy replied. "I love his blonde hair and how it sweeps down over his forehead."

"Well, I think he's the guy for me," I replied wistfully. "But I don't know if he even knows I'm alive. He does talk to me in study hall but barely notices me in the halls or other places."

Lucy came up with a plan. "What if we eat in the cafeteria tomorrow? We can find him and ask to sit with him and see what he says. How can he resist three girls asking to sit with him?"

"Oh, Lucy, would you be that brave?" Ethel said with eyes wide. "He is really cute, and I think he could have any one of the girls in our class. Why do you think he'd want us to sit with him?"

"I think he's a gentleman and would be nice enough to accept our request to sit with him. It's about time we get to know more people in our class," Lucy said with confidence.

"I'm all for that idea! But you girls have to let me sit across from him so I can look into his big blue eyes," I said with enthusiasm.

Soon the bell rang and it was time for us to make our way to class. We had to stop at our lockers first. As we stood at the top of the long staircase that led down one floor to our classrooms, I had an idea how we could get down the stairs lickety-split.

"I know a fast way to get down the stairs," I said as I hitched up my skirt and sat on the wide banister, which made a perfect slide. "Watch this, girls." I was on my way to the first floor, and in no time, I was there and jumped down from the banister, only to be met by the principal, Mr. Anderson.

"Miss Sletten," he said sternly, "that is no way for a young lady to act. You sure aren't like your sister, Edith."

As I slunk away, I thought, *I'm glad I'm not like Edith. She never had any fun.* But I was a little afraid that Mr. Anderson would tell my Papa and that Papa would be very disappointed in me for acting like that, but I thought, *It was fun and I may try it again. Next time I'll just make sure no one is around to see me.*

The next day I wore my best dress and a ribbon in my hair, which I had started to do even though I had very fine, short hair, so the ribbon didn't want to stay in very well. I would realize halfway through the day that I was missing my ribbon and would have to go looking for it.

Sure enough, Royle sat in front of me for study hall and turned around to say hi. Today he said, "Your name is Mary Ellen, isn't it?"

Suddenly, the cat got my tongue and I stared blankly in his big, blue eyes. Luckily, I came to my senses and said timidly, "Yes, Mary Ellen Sletten. And what is your name?" As if I didn't know.

"I'm Royle Johnson, and I'm glad to meet you. Hey, that was a pretty swell trick you did yesterday on the banister. I haven't seen anyone try that before, especially when the principal was standing at the bottom of the stairs."

I was instantly mortified! I had no idea that my heartthrob had seen my acrobatic trick.

I must have turned three shades of red. I was, however, honored that he thought it was a swell trick.

"Well, I don't think I'll try that trick anytime soon," I answered just as the bell rang and he had to turn around and get to work. I continued to look at him. His head was just perfect, so nice, and his hair was combed so neat and clean. I loved to look at his arms from the back. They had some pretty good muscles—must be from working on the farm and he was tanned to perfection.

Before I knew it, the bell was ringing for us to move to our next class. As he stood, he turned and looked down at me with those dreamy blue eyes and said, "Mary Ellen, would you like to join me for lunch today?"

My mouth must have dropped open, but I got ahold of myself and said, "Sure I would! I'll be with my two friends, Lucy and Ethel. Can they sit with us too?" Suddenly, I thought, *Why did I say that?*

Now I know Lucy will dominate the conversation and I won't get a word in edgewise. He asked me to sit with him alone! How can I be so stupid?

"Sure," he said, "the more the merrier. See you at lunch." Then he was gone. He left me sitting there with a dumb look on my face. The teacher came over and said, "Mary Ellen, you will be late for your class if you don't hurry."

The rest of the morning I was in a daze. Royle had asked me to eat lunch with him. All my life's dreams moved before my eyes. We would be married in a lovely ceremony at the Methodist Church. He would whisk me off to a beautiful honeymoon somewhere exotic, and then we would make our home in a beautiful house and fill it up with beautiful children. Just beautiful!

I was suddenly brought back to earth by the teacher calling my name, "Mary Ellen, can you come up front and diagram this sentence for us?"

What sentence? I asked myself. But I knew I had to at least try. I actually liked diagraming sentences, so I confidently strolled up to the front and asked as cool as I could, "What sentence would that be, Miss Bergen?"

"If you were paying attention, you would know what sentence I'm talking about. It's written right here on the black board."

"I'm sorry, Miss Bergen," I said as I began to diagram the sentence. I did it correctly, accepted her praise, and returned to my seat. I was mortified that I had been caught daydreaming. *Shake out of this,* I thought. *Get ahold of yourself. Papa and Mama would kill me if they knew I wasn't paying attention in high school.*

Lunch couldn't come soon enough, and as I met Lucy and Ethel, I said, "let me ask Royle if we can sit with him."

"What?" Lucy said. "Are you brave enough to ask him?"

"Actually," I said with a glint in my eye, "he asked me in study hall this morning to eat lunch with him today. You'll never guess, but he saw me slide down the banister yesterday and he said it was a 'swell trick.' Can you believe that?"

"Well, I guess you don't want to have us tagging along then," Ethel said.

"Oh no, I asked if you two can join us and he said, 'Sure, the more the merrier.' He is so nice."

That lunch was the most memorable lunch I'd ever had. I sat right across from Royle, and Lucy and Ethel sat on either side of me. There were two other boys there, so we were matched up perfectly. I found we had a lot in common. Both of us had grown up on farms, and he had two brothers and a sister. He only lived a couple of miles out of town, so he walked into Canton for high school. He had to be home to help with the milking every day.

Lunch was soon over and the bell was ringing for us to return to our classes. Royle turned to me and said, "I'm happy you sat with me for lunch. Maybe we can do it again soon."

"I would love that," I said as we all turned to go to our classes. What a day! I actually got to eat lunch with the boy of my dreams!

THE HAYRIDE

I WAS WALKING TO CLASS when I turned the corner, and there, right in front of me, stood Royle! All five foot and nine inches of him. Because I was only about five foot two inches, I had to look up to his face. Royle was good-looking, but not a dreamboat as some were classified. He had light, sun-bleached, wavy hair, and a small piece of it fell down on his forehead. He had the dreamiest eyes of anyone I had ever met. They were dark blue like the ocean, and he had the longest eyelashes I had ever seen—way too long for a boy, but that was part of his dreamy look. Because of all the farm work he had done over the summer, he was well-built, with just enough muscles on his arms. Not like a professional weightlifter or anything, but just enough.

"Well, if it isn't the fearless half-pint who dared to slide the banister," he said in his starting-to-change male voice.

I immediately turned three shades of red, which I hated! "Hi Royle," I said, trying to keep my breathlessness at bay. Then I had nothing. What could I say? There were things I would've liked to have said like, "You are the cutest boy I have ever met," or "Where did you get those long eyelashes?" But there I stood, with my mouth hanging open, staring up into his blue, blue eyes. I went limp and tongue-tied.

"Well, hello to you too, Mary Ellen. I've been looking for you," he said with his partially bass voice.

"You have?" I responded weakly. I just didn't have any good comeback at that moment.

"Yes," he continued, "I want to ask you to go with me to the freshman hayride next Saturday night. I know you usually go home on weekends, but maybe you could ask to stay in town this week-end. My Dad is bringing our hay rack in and a team of horses to pull it with. Everyone in our class will be there, and it will be a great way to get to know everyone What do you think?"

I could hardly contain my excitement, but I didn't want to act too forward, so I said, "I'll ask Papa and Mama if I can stay in town and go to the hayride. I don't know if they'd be alright with it if they knew I was going with a boy," I said. I felt the redness creeping up from my neck. "But I don't have to tell them that, I guess, just that it's a class social."

"Okay," he said with a wink. "It will be our little secret." Then he was off, and I was left standing in the hallway feeling very warm and fuzzy.

The rest of the day was a blur as I was walking on cloud nine with excitement. I could hardly wait to call Mama and Papa that evening and ask about staying in town this weekend and going to the class hayride. I would be very careful not to mention anything about Royle, as I'm sure they would say I was way too young to have a date. But I didn't think it was a true date, like when you go with someone to a movie, just the two of you. This was a class party, and I would just happen to be sitting next to Royle Johnson the whole time. The thought made my palms sweaty and my heart race.

That afternoon as I was leaving school, I saw Ethel walking toward our home, so I ran to catch up with her. I could hardly stand still as I told her my news. "Guess what happened to me today?"

Ethel replied dryly, "What, did you get an A+ on your test?"

"No, something way more exciting! I got asked to the freshman hayride by someone. Guess who?" By this time, I was jumping up and down waiting for her to guess.

"Well, by your reaction…don't tell me it's Royle?"

"Yes!" I squealed. "He asked me right in the hallway when I was on my way to class. I was so dumb, I didn't say yes right away, because I have to ask my parents if I can stay in town this weekend and go to the hayride."

"Do you think your parents will let you go on a date?" Ethel asked.

"Weeeeell, I have my doubts, but I don't have to tell them I'm going with a boy—only that it's a freshman social for our class to get to know each other. That wouldn't be lying, would it?" I was already feeling uneasy about leaving that part out when asking my parents.

"Remember what the Bible says, 'Be sure your sins will find you out,'" Ethel said, which made me feel even more convicted about not being truthful with my folks.

My big, beautiful balloon had burst! I knew I had to be truthful when I asked Mama and Papa about the hayride. The rest of the way home I felt like my feet weighed a thousand pounds. I would wait until after supper to call Mama and Papa. They shouldn't be too surprised, as the last few times I had been home I had talked about Royle and how he had become my friend.

That night, after the supper dishes were all cleaned up, I went to the phone on the wall. I had asked Mrs. Hicks if I might be able to call my parents to see if I could stay the weekend for the hayride. My knees were shaking and my hands were sweating as I reached for the receiver and put it to my ear. I turned the crank handle on the side, one short and two long rings. It continued to ring until finally I heard Edith's voice on the line.

"Hi Edith, this is Mary Ellen. How is everything going at home?" I was trying to be calm, like I was calling just to catch up, not to talk about the most exciting thing that had happened in my whole life.

"Oh, things are about the same here. Do you want to talk to Papa? He's right here."

"Yes, I do have something to ask him." As I waited for him to come to the phone, I pictured him standing tall in the pulpit at church. He was a lay preacher, which meant that he would help out with preaching in our church and others, if the pastor was away. This didn't help me with my dilemma—whether to tell him about Royle or not.

Suddenly, I heard his familiar voice on the other end. "How is my Little Tyke?" He had called me that since I was born, but now I really didn't like that nickname anymore. Especially since I was practically the shortest person in our class, and I was about to ask him if I could go out with a boy. Not just any boy, but the cutest boy in the freshman class, at least in my opinion.

"Hi, Papa, I wish you wouldn't call me 'Little Tyke' anymore. You know I'm growing up". Then I felt kind of bad for saying that but continued with what I had called about. "The freshman class is having a hayride this Saturday night." I took a big breath and tried to swallow, but my mouth was too dry. "Well, I have been asked to go with a friend and I would need to stay in town this weekend so I can go." It all just tumbled out, but there, I said it. At least most of it.

Papa replied with the question I knew he would ask. "Who is the friend that you'll be going with? Do we know her?"

Oh, boy! Now what? "Well, Papa, it isn't actually a girl friend, it is a boy friend who asked me to go with him." By now my hands were shaking so badly I could hardly hold the receiver.

There was a long, long silence on the other end of the line. At first, I thought maybe he'd hung up on me, or that he'd dropped the phone receiver, but soon he came back on.

"Well, Little T…, I mean, Mary Ellen, this is quite a development. I'm glad you came to us to ask. You could've gone without our knowing about it. I'm proud of you for asking. Your Ma and I have talked about this topic before, when your sister wanted to date, and we decided that fourteen is just too young to go on dates with boys."

My heart sank and my throat started to close off, as I was about ready to burst out crying.

Papa continued, "Your mother and I think it's okay for you to stay in town this weekend to go to the hayride, but we think you're just too young to go with a boy. You can go with Lucy and your other friends and have a good time. I'm not saying that you can't even talk to a boy—that would be impossible—but we don't want to you to get too serious over a boy quite yet. Is he Royle Johnson?

Maybe when you are sixteen or seventeen you can go on a date. How about that?" he said and then waited for me to answer.

By now my lower lip was quivering as I tried to compose myself. "Papa, I understand and thank you for allowing me to go," I said through my tears. "I'll tell Royle that I can't go with him, but that I'll be there with my girlfriends. Papa, I love you, and tell Mama that I love her too and will miss seeing you all this weekend."

"We love you too, Mary Ellen, and we trust you to obey our wishes. We will see you the next weekend. And soon it will be Thanksgiving break, and you'll be home for that. Bye now."

"Bye-bye, Papa," I whispered as I hung the receiver up on its cradle. I could hold back the tears no more. I ran upstairs to the room I was sharing with Lucy and threw myself on my bed and sobbed. My heart was broken, and I didn't want to face tomorrow. What would I tell Royle? How could I tell him that my parents thought I was too young to go out with a boy? This definitely was the worst day of my entire life!

Suddenly, I realized that Ethel was sitting in the armchair watching me in my hour of trouble. I sat up, dried my tears, looked at her and said, "Now that my life is over, what should I do?"

"Oh, Mary Ellen, did they say you had to come home this weekend, or can you stay and go to the hayride, just not with a boy?"

"They said I can go to the hayride, but that I had to go with my girlfriends. They said I was too young to go out with a boy and maybe when I'm sixteen or seventeen, I could go with a boy. Can you imagine? Why, that is two or three years from now! All the good boys will be taken by then, especially Royle. What can I tell Royle tomorrow? How can I break it to him that my parents won't let me go with him?"

"You'll still have a great time at the hayride. Remember, Royle will still be there and you can still talk to him at school like you've been doing. I think you can have a lot of fun just with the girls. We don't need any old boys to have a good time," Ethel said to encourage me.

"I guess you're right, and Papa and Mama are probably right too. I have a lot of years to look for the right boy and when I see him, I will know he's the one for me," I said.

The next day at lunch Lucy and I sat with Royle. I was tongue-tied trying to get my nerve up to tell him my answer. But finally, I turned to him and put my hand on his arm as I said, "My parents don't want me going with you to the hayride. It isn't that they don't like you; it's just that they think I'm too young to go with boys. I hope you're not too disappointed."

Royle looked a little crestfallen. Then he said, "To tell you the truth, my parents didn't want me to take a girl to the hayride either. They said the same thing your parents said. I guess I should've asked them before I asked you to go with me. I was trying to figure out a way to let you down easy, but now we both have the same excuse. Will you sit with me some time at the hayride? Because my Pop will be there, I have to be careful it doesn't look like we're on a date."

"I would love to have you sit by me some of the time. It's going to be a swell time, I just know it," I said.

When Saturday night came, I wore my new blue-and-cream-colored wool skirt that Mama had made for me for winter and a cream-colored sweater. I wore something under the sweater so that I didn't have to wear a coat. I did wear my hat and mittens, and, of course, my sturdy shoes. You can't go climbing around on a hay rack unless you have good shoes. Ethel and I walked to the school where the hay rack was waiting. Several of our other friends came running up as we arrived, and we found where we wanted to sit. As I was contemplating how I should get up on the hay rack, I heard a male voice behind me. "Need a little lift up?"

It was Royle. "Yes, I guess it is a little hard to climb up with a skirt on. After this summer I didn't think I would ever be excited to get on a hay rack again." He bent down and put his hands together and I stepped into his hands and up I went.

The night was a perfect, warm harvest moon kind of night, and the stars were sparkling in the sky like diamonds. I was happy, very happy, that I had parents who loved me and took care of me. I had friends to share things with, and I had a boy friend who gave me a different perspective to life. I looked up into the night sky as the horses pulled the rack along the country road and said a little prayer to God for giving me life and everything I had. I even got to sit with Royle next to me for about a mile. Life was good!

GOOD OL' SUMMERTIME

T HE SUMMER AFTER MY freshman year was a hard one. Crops were still pretty much non-existent, and Papa worked very hard to keep hay going so we could feed our milk cows. Hay was about the only thing that would grow and could be harvested. Things were very bad all over the mid-west, and there were some places in South Dakota that couldn't even grow hay to feed the cattle. We felt very blessed that we were able to grow hay, and Mama's garden did fairly well with the water we would carry from the well.

When we weren't in the fields, I was able to go stay with my Aunt Mary. She taught me so much and really encouraged me to continue in school and get good grades so I could have a good job when I graduated.

"Aunt Mary," I said one day as we were making wild plum jelly, "I don't see why I have to study so hard and get good grades in school. I will just find a man and get married, and he'll take care of me and

*Mary Ellen (right) with sister, Edith (left) on
Mary Ellen's high school graduation. 1936*

our family. I just need to know how to cook, clean, and take care of kids. I plan on having a lot of kids so they can play with each other."

"Mary Ellen, you can't count on that. There's many a slip twixt cup and lip. Look at your sister. I don't think she'll ever marry. Luckily, she is needed to take care of your mother and Grandpa. I found out how important an education is. If something happens to Charley, God forbid, I can support myself. In this day and age, a family can't always rely on the husband to be the only bread winner."

I thought about that as I licked my sticky fingers. My Aunt Mary is a very smart woman, and I guess she knows what she is talking about, even though I wondered what she meant about the slip of the cup. "I guess you're right. I'll try and do better next year in school," I said.

"Do you have any idea what you might want to do when you graduate from high school?" Aunt Mary asked as she spun the jar lids on tight.

"I think I would like to be a secretary. I took typing this year, and I got pretty good at it. My teacher said I have the aptitude for typing. There are a lot of places who need secretaries, like schools and colleges. I have seen the secretaries in the courthouse typing up a storm. That would be a nice place to work," I responded as Aunt Mary placed the jars of jelly in a water bath to seal them. I could hardly wait to try out the plum jelly on some homemade bread.

"I think you should think about being a teacher," Aunt Mary said. "They make a better salary than a secretary. You could teach typing and office-related classes."

Now that was something I hadn't thought about. But that would take four years of college, and I didn't know if Mama and Papa would be able to pay for it. I decided I would ask my typing teacher, Miss McMillian, if she likes teaching and where she went to college.

The next day I went off to Bible camp in Hudson, which was always a highlight of my summer. It was fun to see all the friends I had made from other years. We made crafts, swam in the river, played games, and learned Bible stories. I was sad when it was time to go home that summer, but I looked forward to returning to high school in the fall, as I missed seeing Royle terribly. I looked at what Royle had written in my little school autograph book and dreamt about seeing him in September.

Dear Mary Ellen,
When Columbus discovered America in 1492
I discovered something better
When I discovered you.

Your Friend, Royle A. Johnson

Back at home after Bible Camp, I helped Papa with the hay and the milking. I always liked the time I spent with Papa out in the barn in the morning before anyone else was awake. We had some good talks there.

"Papa," I said one cool morning, "I think I want to marry a farmer. I love the farm so much and I can't imagine not living on a farm. It is a lot of hard work, but it's so peaceful and quiet out here, with only the sounds of the cows mooing and the horses moving about in their stalls. It sounds like they're ready for a good day's work in the field."

"The farm is a great place to live, even though it's been hard the last few years with this drought. I always have hopes that next year will be better," Papa said. "That's the way it is when you're a farmer. You take the bad with the good. I always have faith that God will take care of us, and he always does. We may not have much, but we have each other, and God provides for our daily needs."

I suddenly realized my kitty, Tiger, was standing next to me meowing. "Oh, Tiger, you have been so faithful and patient. Look at you, waiting for your squirt of milk. Here you go," I said as I squirted her in the face and mouth. My aim wasn't as good as Papa's. "I'll give you more after we're done with milking." Tiger had been my kitty since I was eight years old. She had many litters, which kept us supplied with cats to keep the mice away.

One cool summer morning, as I was helping Edith with the garden, I looked up as I heard someone shout, "Hello!"

"Elmer!" I cried and ran to the driveway as he rode up on his bicycle. "What in the world, did you ride here all the way from Sioux City? It has to be sixty miles!"

"Yup, I started out real early this morning. It took me about five hours to get here. It's a real nice ride though, and I asked my Pa if I could come visit you folks. I thought I could help around the farm for a week or so," Elmer said as he got off his bicycle.

"We would love to have you, and I know Papa can use you in the field. We're making hay now," I said as I gave him a big hug. He was one of my favorite cousins. His Dad, Ben, and my Mama were brother and sister. They visited us often in the summer.

Mama came out of the house to call us in for dinner and saw Elmer standing in the driveway. "Why, Elmer Bixby! What are you doing here?" She acted surprised, but later I found out that Uncle Ben had called Papa to see if it was okay for Elmer to come spend some time with us. It seems he needed to get him out of his hair for a while.

Papa came out of the barn and slapped Elmer on the back. "Why, it's Elmer! My, you have grown since the last time I saw you. How old are you now?"

"I'll be in the eighth grade, but Pa thought I was finally old enough to make the trip here. We thought you could use some male help around the farm," he said as he puffed up his chest to look larger.

"Well, I certainly could use some help, and I'm sure Mary Ellen won't turn down help when it comes to making hay in the heat of the day. Come on into the house. You're just in time for dinner," Papa said as we all walked toward the house.

"I was counting on making it here by dinnertime, and after that long bike ride, I'm hungry as a heifer, and my rump can use a little rest," Elmer replied, acting like he knew what a heifer was, even though he lived in town. I guessed Uncle Ben had clued him in on what it was like to live on a farm and thought he could use an education on working hard.

He was a good help and caught on to milking right away. It was great to have another two hands to do the milking, and he learned how to pitch the hay up onto the hay rack with ease.

After his first day pitching hay, he said at suppertime, "Wow, I think I'll be sore tomorrow. My arms feel like noodles." Sure enough the next day, he could hardly move his arms they were so sore. Papa let him ride up on the hay wagon and simply move the hay around so it would be distributed evenly. We had a great time together and the two weeks passed quickly.

A much tanner and more muscular Elmer rode out of our farmyard early one morning. I thought he'll be able to make the trip home a little faster, as he had built some muscles on his legs. We stood in the road and waved at him as he sped off and over the hill. "Bye, Elmer!" I yelled. "Don't forget to write!" It had been a great summer, and I was ready to go back to school in a couple of weeks. I was a little sad that the summer was coming to an end, but excited to get back to school and all my friends, and, of course, to Royle.

THE TYPING TEST

IT WAS MY FIRST day as a sophomore! I was excited and a little nervous about seeing Royle again. Ethel and I were settled back at Mrs. Hicks' house, and we had discussed all the classes we planned to take this year.

"I'm going to take typing again this year," I told her the night before. "Miss Millian told me last year that I had the aptitude to do well in typing. I think it's so fun to see how fast your fingers can fly. I'm going to ask my Papa for a typewriter for Christmas this year."

"It's okay, but I like math and algebra better," Ethel said as we were putting our pajamas on and getting ready for bed.

It will be hard to sleep tonight thinking about school starting tomorrow, I thought as I waited for sleep to come. I knew I was going to dream about Royle.

The next day we were up early, had our breakfast, and tidied our room before we walked to school. It was a warm fall day, and I remembered the day about a year ago when Royle asked me to the freshman hayride. I couldn't wait to get to school to see if he would sit in front of me again.

Lucy and I greeted all our friends outside the school and went in to find our lockers. It was great being back in the school halls again, bustling with students greeting each other. Now there was a new class of freshmen. I remember how I felt last year on my first day of high school, but did I look that scared? I tried to smile at them and help them if they needed help finding their locker. Wow! They all looked so young!

The bell rang, and it was time to get to our homeroom. My heart was beating fast in anticipation of seeing Royle. I found my seat, which was a different one from last year. *Where is Royle?* I thought as I scanned the room. Then I saw him. He had grown at least a couple inches over the summer, and he was tan and even more muscular than I remember. Then I saw *her*, Mae Pearson. She was standing next to him, and they were talking. He sat in a desk next to hers. They continued to talk until the bell rang and we had to be quiet, but I saw them giving each other glances once in a while. I became so angry! How could he not even notice me sitting a few rows back? Just then, he glanced around the room. When he saw me, he waved, smiled, and then turned his attention back to Mae. Well, at least he knows I'm still alive.

Soon we were going to our first classes. I made my way to the English room and almost bumped into Royle.

"Why, Mary Ellen," he said as we stood next to each other. My knees went weak, and I didn't know what to say. "I think you've grown over the summer," he said. Then he went to his desk and I found mine.

Our desks were not close at all, but I had a good view of him from where I sat. Then I remembered my promise to Papa and Aunt Mary that I would buckle down and get better grades. *Snap out of it,* I said to myself. Then I forced myself to concentrate on the teacher and what she was saying, but I couldn't help but glance at Royle a few times. Each time I caught myself, I would snap back to listening mode. This was going to be tough, but I promised Papa and Aunt Mary that I would get good grades, and I will if it kills me!

When class was over, I happened to be leaving at the same time Royle was. I swallowed hard and tried to get my courage up to say something to him. "Well, Royle, how was your summer"? I asked as I jockeyed my books in my arms.

"Oh, pretty good, I guess," he said as we walked down the hall. "It was a hot one, and crops were pretty bad again. Don't know what will happen if we don't get rain one of these years." Suddenly, he saw Mae. He turned to me and said, "Well, shortie, I better get going. I'm glad you had a good summer, too. See you later." Then he was gone.

Shortie! I might be short, but I am mighty. I remember when I was about five or six, our country school came into Canton for field days. There were races of all kinds. I begged Mama to let me run in one of the races. She thought I was too little, but I kept pestering her until she agreed to let me run. I took off from the starting line like a shot, and my short little legs were going for all I was worth, but I was left far behind. I could hear the crowd cheering at the top of their lungs. I didn't stop until I had crossed the finish line, much later than everyone else. But I guess they felt sorry for me, because they gave me a ribbon which I proudly held out for Mama to see as I ran back to where she was watching.

"Why, Mary Ellen, you got a ribbon," Mama said and gave me a big hug.

I had that stick-to-it kind of attitude. Papa always said, "If you don't succeed the first time, try, try again." So, I wasn't going to give up so easily on Royle.

My next class was typing. I loved typing and my teacher Miss Millian. She made it so fun and really made you want to keep trying to get faster and more accurate. It didn't matter if you could type like the wind if there were mistakes on half the page. It is easy to do if you don't get your fingers on the home row—right hand on ASDF, left hand on JKLsemicolon. That was where you started out every time you started typing. From there, you learned where the other letters were on the keyboard. Last year I was pretty slow and made a lot of mistakes. This year I was going to try to be the best typist in my class, as I wanted to get into college.

"Class," Miss Millian said loudly so she could be heard over everyone talking, "we will now have a timed test. Everyone quiet down. I know it's been a while since many of you have used a type-writer, but this is just to see where you are at the beginning of the year so I can see how much you improve during the year. Now remember to make sure your hands are on the home row on the keyboard." We all had our books propped open to the page we were to type. This was the first time we had a timed test, and I anticipated getting off like a flash when the bell rang.

Miss Millan continued: "You will have one minute to type as fast as you can, but remember, errors will be taken off your time. You may start when the bell rings and stop when it rings again. You shouldn't type even one more letter after the bell rings…. Get ready…"

Ding! The bell rang, and we were off like racehorses off the starting line, click-clacking along at a ferocious speed. You could hear the dinging of everyone's carriage return as we were intent on getting the most words on the page. My fingers were flying, and when the bell rang, I had almost finished the whole page.

"Give us another one," I said to Miss Millian. I was like a prize racehorse chomping at the bit to run.

"Okay, please turn to the next page," Miss Millan instructed. That page had longer words and more punctuation in it, which would make speed harder to achieve, but I was up to the task. I was poised on my home row, waiting for the bell.

As soon as I heard it, I was off, my fingers flying and throwing the carriage return. I could tell I wasn't making as much progress on this page as the last one. When the bell rang, everyone stopped. I looked at the page in my typewriter and in shock thought, *Something must be wrong.*

Half the words weren't even words at all. *What happened?* I was so disappointed in myself. I must not have had my hands in the right place on the keyboard when I started, or maybe I didn't get my fingers back on the home row when I threw the carriage. I typed fast, but the words were all wrong. After that, I learned to always take the time to check to make sure my hands were in the right place on the keyboard before starting to type.

"Don't worry, Mary Ellen," Miss Millian said after class. "That's a common mistake. You will get it and your speed is excellent. Just keep practicing."

I just have to get a typewriter at home so I can practice there too, I thought to myself. *I will talk to Papa about it next time I go home.*

The first day of my sophomore year was an exciting and disappointing one. But I had the whole year to look forward to. *What things would I learn in school, and what would become of my love for Royle?* I thought as I walked slowly home.

GRANDPA'S REMINISCING

MY GRANDPA SLETTEN LOVED to tell stories about the past— about his life when his family came to "Dakota" from Wisconsin and about growing up on the prairie. He told the stories as if he was re-living everything.

I loved to go to Grandpa's house as it was not far from where I was boarding. Usually, we played rook or snap, but this Saturday, as I looked at the pictures on the wall in the dining room, I wanted to know more about the faces I saw.

"Grandpa," I started, "how did you and Grandma meet?"

He got this faraway look in his eyes, and I thought I saw a softening as he started to tell me about it.

"Our family came from Wisconsin when I was thirteen," he said. "It was quite a trip as I recall. All us kids were along except for my older sister, Caroline, as she was already married.

I knew right then he wasn't going to just answer my question but wanted to go back to the beginning. I settled in for a long evening, listening to his cracking voice.

"Well, it was in 1876 when we started out by covered wagons pulled by teams of oxen," he continued. "Some of my cousins also came along, as their father had passed away and they wanted to have an adventure. My oldest brother, Ole, was twenty, then Martin was eighteen, Edward was fifteen, I was thirteen, Thomas was ten, Sam was eight, and my youngest sister, Ellen—we called her Alena—was only four years old. My cousins who came were about the age of Ole and Martin, so they helped a lot driving the teams. Us little kids who were big enough walked most of the way. Only Alena got to be in the wagon with Mama. My Papa was going to get enough land in Dakota so all of us could have farms of our own when we got old enough. Ole and Martin were able to get their own homestead right away," he said.

"So, Grandpa," I interrupted, "when are you going to tell me about how you met Grandma?"

"Hold your horses, Little Tyke, I'm getting to that."

I hated it when he called me Little Tyke, especially since I was in high school. Then he had to stop to take a big sip of his coffee, dunk his sugar cookie in his cup, and take a bite of the cookie, before he continued.

"Yup, that was a long hard trip for all of us. I didn't think we'd ever get to Dakota. But finally, we crossed over from Iowa to Dakota and then we knew it wouldn't be long."

He gazed off in the distance as if he was seeing Dakota for the first time again. Then, he continued. "We stopped for the day at a farm north of Canton, and the man there said he was looking for a boy to watch his cattle herd and wondered if Papa and Mama could spare one of their boys for the summer."

"So, you lived right here in Canton then too"? I asked.

"Not in Canton, it was a farm north of here. I was a good herder, because it had been my job to take care of the cattle while they grazed in the pasture back in Wisconsin. There were no fences back then, so they needed to have someone out in the field to make sure they didn't stray too far from home," he said.

"Wow, Grandpa, what did you do all day out in the field? I bet you got lonesome with only the cows to talk to," I said.

"I did get lonesome for my family, but the man, Mr. Nelson, had shown me the horse I would use and said if I did a good job, I would get a salary plus I could keep the horse. The horse kept me company, and it was much easier to move cattle that way."

"What was your horse's name?" I asked. "I bet something like Boots or Kicker."

"It was a pretty Palomino that had a white face and boots, but I didn't call him Boots, I called him Pal. He was my Pal for a long time, and Papa said he would also be a good workhorse when he got a little older," Grandpa said.

"Was that your first horse, Grandpa?" I asked.

"No, I had a horse in Wisconsin for about four years. His name was Fancy. He was a good horse, but he was too old to make the trip to Dakota, so we left him with my sister, Caroline. I hated to let him go, but I knew he'd be taken care of and her kids would ride him. Well, I better get on with the rest of this story or we'll be here all night," Grandpa said.

"I need to be back to the Hicks' by eight, so we only have a couple hours left, but I want to hear all about it, so don't leave anything out. Maybe someday I can write a story about your life, Grandpa," I said.

"It would be a fine story, little…I mean, Mary Ellen. The way you can speed type, it wouldn't take you long at all," he said. "So, where was I, oh yes, I had a job which was the best thing that ever happened to me, except for the day I met your Grandma. I could spend the day out on the prairie with my horse and watch cattle. Some days it was pretty hot, but I would find a tree and sit under it. That's where I found the soft stone that I carved this little Bible from."

Grandpa slowly got up from his rocker and walked over to the table by the big window and picked up the carved Bible that I had seen there many times. "This is one I am particularly proud of because of the color variation. It looks like the spine of the Bible is a different color than the cover." As he came back to his chair with it, he asked, "Mary Ellen, would you like this Bible?"

"Oh, Grandpa, I would love to have it. I love feeling how smooth it is and knowing that you made it makes it a treasure I'll keep forever," I said.

"I want to carve something on the front first. When I get it finished, I'll give it to you," he said.

"Well, back to the story. That summer went by fast and in the fall, I was back with my family. I was amazed at the amount of land Papa was able to get for us, and for Ole and Martin. He had a piece of land picked out for me too, so when I was eighteen, I'd have a homestead. Ole had built a sod house and put up a small barn for his livestock and horses. He had managed to turn quite a bit of sod to plant corn, and, of course, he put up hay from the prairie grass. Papa built a large barn, and on one end was our living quarters.

It was warm and cozy, but when the wind and snow blew, it was downright cold! But we managed, and soon it was spring and I could get a good look at my homestead land," he said.

Again, Grandpa looked off into the distance with a wistful look on his face.

"Was that when you met Grandma?" I asked. I didn't think he would ever get to that part of the story.

"No, I didn't meet her for three more years, when I was eighteen," he said. "One day, I was out working on a barn I was building on my homestead when a wagon drove up with a man and lady and two little boys. The two boys were the cutest kids, and they hid behind their mom's skirt. The man's name was Peter Anderson, and he had a homestead about five miles from my place. It was a very sad situation; Peter had just found out he was dying of cancer. When Peter was telling me this, I saw the wife dabbing a hanky at her eyes, and I could tell she was fighting back tears. My heart went out to them, and as I looked at her and their small boys, I almost burst out crying myself. Peter asked me if I could help him on his farm, as he was afraid that he would not be able to do it himself. He milked a few cows; he could manage that himself, but he needed help with the fieldwork. I told him I'd come over the next day and look over things and give him my answer. When they left, I couldn't get those little boys out of my mind. Their eyes looked so innocent and scared by what was going on. I decided right then that I would do what ever was needed for this little family."

"What was the ladies name, Grandpa?" I asked.

"Her name was Isabelle, Isabelle Anderson," he said.

"Grandpa? Did she have the same name as Grandma?" I asked.

"She is your Grandma, Mary Ellen," he said, as he took out his big red handkerchief and blew his nose loudly, dabbing a few tears from his eyes. He took another sip of his coffee, which was cold by now, and said, "Well, that's all for tonight. You better get going to Mrs. Hicks.'"

"But, Grandpa," I objected, "I want to find out what happened. How is she my Grandma? She was married when you met her," I said.

"Here's what happened," he said. "Isabelle's husband, Peter, did die from cancer about six months after she gave birth to a daughter, Mary. That baby girl is your Aunt Mary. Peter had asked me, when he knew he didn't have much time left, to take care of his family when he was gone. I had grown fond of the children, and Isabelle was a wonderful mother and wife. I kept my promise and looked after them for the next year. In that time, Isabelle and I fell in love and were married. That's how it all happened and how you came to be, because we had your Papa, John, as our first child. Now you better get going," he said.

As I walked back to Mrs. Hicks', I looked up into the stars and thought about what a hero my Grandpa was. He had rescued that little family and made them his own. I knew Aunt Mary thought of Grandpa as her father, but I also had more questions. What happened to the two little boys? I had heard Papa and Aunt Mary talk about her brothers, and I knew they had died, but I didn't know what happened. That is something I would ask Grandpa next time I saw him. I had such a feeling of thankfulness, and I said right then, "Thank you, God, for giving me such a wonderful Grandpa."

22

HOME IS BEST

M Y SECOND YEAR IN high school went by quickly. I had given up on Royle after he asked me to go to a dance with him. I knew that would not go over well with Mama and Papa since Methodists didn't dance. After that, he hardly talked to me.

I was concentrating on keeping my grades up, because I really wanted to go to college and become a teacher. I had talked to an older girl at church that was going to Dakota Wesleyan in Mitchell, South Dakota. It sounded like a wonderful school, and they had a two-year teaching degree which would allow me to get out on my own sooner.

Before I knew it, I was a junior in high school and could see the reality of going to college on the horizon, except for the drought. That always put a damper on things. We really didn't have it too bad, and Mama always had a large garden and put up quarts and quarts of garden produce. We had enough hay to feed our few cows, so they gave us plenty of milk, cream, and butter to sell in town. Our chickens were laying like mad, which gave us an abundant egg production. But Papa still had to be careful with what little money we had. He had been doing some lay preaching also, which brought in some money.

In November we had a terrible snowstorm that lasted for days. I was unable to go home on the weekend as I usually did, so I was stuck in town for three weeks. There was no mail service and most phone lines in the county were down. I worried about Mama, Papa, and Edith out on the farm. What if Papa got lost going out to milk the cows? What if Mama got sick and the doctor couldn't get out to see her? I was thankful that Edith was there with them. She had a level head and could help Papa and take care of Mama.

Finally, after three weeks the road south of the farm was opened and the men from the neighborhood brought sacks and rode the snowplow to town to pick up mail and groceries. Papa came to pick me up, and soon we were driving home. I was never so happy to be going home.

The road looked very strange and different than it usually did. The snow was piled up on each side of the road higher than the top of the car. It was only one lane, which made it a little difficult if you met someone head on.

"What happens if we meet someone coming the other way?" I asked Papa as we drove the ten miles to our farm.

"The snowplow has cleared some driveways, so one of the cars will have to back up until it can pull into a driveway and let the other car pass. I haven't met anyone so far. I don't think there are a lot of people out and about," Papa replied. "This was a doozie of a storm. I remember my Papa telling me about the bad snowstorm in 1888. That's how I learned about tying a rope between the house and the barn. That came in handy. I was able to make it out to the barn after digging out the front door and walking on top of the snow to the barn, where I then dug out the barn door. There were a few mornings the old milk cows were bellerin' pretty loud before I got to them. The snow was up to the top of the fences around the cow yard. I had to shovel around the fence line so the cows couldn't walk out of the yard. There were places where the snow was so deep in the trees that you could walk up to a tree and look down on the birds' nests. It's a lot of snow but we sure can use this moisture."

It was so wonderful to get home that day. Mama was up and Edith was helping her cook supper. It seemed like I had been away from home for a year.

Edith and I had forged a new relationship. She no longer looked at me as a bother, but would talk to me as an equal. We had many nice talks when I was home.

"Well, it's time to get the milking done before supper," Papa said.

"I'll help you, Papa. I love milking the cows and have actually missed them," I said as we put on our heavy work coats and boots. After I grabbed and lit my little lantern, we headed out to the barn. Papa had shoveled a path to the barn, and the snow was up to my waist on both sides. "Wow, Papa," I exclaimed, "the snow is so deep. How did you get all this shoveled?"

"Edith helped me some, and the neighbor came over and helped a lot. I couldn't have done it by myself," he said as we entered the barn. We heard the cows outside the door impatiently waiting to be let in and milked.

When we opened the door, there were the six cows. They mooed loudly when they saw us, and one by one they entered the barn and found the stanchion, where they stood to be milked. The barn cats were there also, waiting for their supper. Tiger was leading the little group. She rubbed up against my legs and purred loudly as if to say, "I sure missed you."

Supper that night seemed exceptionally wonderful, even though it was the 'usual fare,' as Mama said. We talked long after our plates were emptied. When it was time to do the dishes, Edith and I took over to let Papa and Mama go to their easy chairs in the living room. Mama sat in her rocker, and Papa sat in his big leather chair which could accommodate his six-foot frame. He loved that chair ever since they purchased it for Christmas a few years ago. We'd had Mama's rocker for many years. She had rocked both Edith and me in it when we were babies. I remember sitting on her lap and being rocked at night. She would read to me, and I would soon be asleep.

Edith and I busied ourselves clearing the dishes and getting them washed, dried, and put away in the cupboard.

"Edith, I have missed you so much these last three weeks. I thought about some of the talks we've had and wished I could've at least called you or gotten a letter from you," I said.

"I know," Edith replied, "I missed you too and wished the mail would go through so we could send letters back and forth telling what we were doing. How is school this year?"

"School is easier for me this year, I think because I've given up on boys and I'm concentrating more on my classes and getting good grades. After this year, I only have one more year until I graduate and then I hope to go to college, maybe Dakota Wesleyan in Mitchell," I told her with excitement in my voice.

"If you stick it out, you'll make it. I know Mama and Papa are proud of you and the grades you are bringing home. Are you still thinking you want to be a secretary?" Edith asked, as she hung the dishtowel on the warm oven door to dry.

"I'm thinking now that maybe I want to be a teacher. I could teach the secretarial subjects. This year I'm taking shorthand, and it's really fun to learn," I said. "My friends and I use it to pass notes to each other in class so no one can understand what we're saying. Dakota Wesleyan has a two-year teaching degree, so I figure I could be out on my own in a little over three years, but things could get in the way of that. Maybe I will meet the man of my dreams and get married and start the big family I want," I said with a smile.

"I hope all your dreams come true for you, Mary Ellen," Edith said. "I had big dreams when I graduated from high school and started college, but those dreams vanished after trying to teach for a year and a half. I just couldn't do it," she said wistfully. "Now my life is staying home, taking care of Mama and Papa. That's what old maids do, right?"

"Edith, you're not an old maid. Look at Aunt Mary. She didn't get married until she was in her forties! So, there is hope for you. Haven't you had anyone who you thought you could marry? Maybe in high school or college?" I asked.

"Mary Ellen, I never told anyone about this, but there was a boy I dated in college that I thought I was in love with," Edith said. "His name was Grant. He was a very nice man and treated me so special, but I don't think he was in love with me, at least he never told me. I never told him how I felt…I thought the man should say it first. When I graduated and came back home to teach, I said goodbye to him and that was the last time I ever saw him. I was heartbroken. Then when the teaching job went bad, I kind of had a little breakdown and had to come home. Those were terrible years, and I decided that I would never let another man hurt me like he did. I'm content now being home and caring for Mama. It gives my life purpose, and Papa needs my help also."

"I'm so thankful for you being here and taking care of things. I don't know if I could do it, but you just seem to know what to do," I said as I gave her a big hug. It felt good to hug my sister. We have had a lot of differences between us in our childhood, but now we seemed to be on common ground.

After being away from my family for three weeks, I had a new perspective about them. I loved them even more and appreciated all they did to keep our family strong and healthy. Papa worked so hard, and someday I hope he will be able to get back to preaching, which is his real love. I pray every day that Mama will be with us many more years, but I know that won't happen. Someday, I'll have to say goodbye to her and then to Papa. My heart broke when I thought about it. For now, I will never take my family for granted.

As I looked forward to the coming years, I prayed that night I would have a family that loved and cared for each other. "Thank you, God, for giving me my family," I whispered in the dark as I snuggled down in my comfy bed. Home is the best!

GRADUATION AND WEDDING ANNIVERSARY

I COULD HARDLY BELIEVE IT. Soon I would be graduating from high school. It seemed like just yesterday that I was walking to Pleasant Ridge, holding on to Edith's hand, starting first grade. Mama and Papa said the same thing. "Where have the years gone?" Mama lamented. "I feel so blessed to see both my girls graduate from high school."

Mama had been ill most of the year. We had called the doctor to come see her several times.

"She's having small strokes," the doctor said. "It's just a matter of time before she has a large one that she won't recover from. I'm sorry to give you this bad news. There's nothing more I can do for her. Keep her comfortable and enjoy the good days you have with her," he told Papa after he came out of the bedroom so Mama could not hear.

Papa looked at his hands, and I saw a tear run down his face. Mama was everything to him. He had cared for her through sickness and rejoiced during times of happiness. I wondered how he would take losing her. I wondered how all of us would. She was the glue that held us together. The sure, strong voice we heard in times of trouble. Always encouraging us and always leading the way. *This can't be happening,* I thought to myself. Mama's only fifty years old. *That's too young to die.*

I started to cry and then I noticed Edith by my side with tears in her eyes. She put her arms around me, and we both cried together.

That was in March of 1936, but by spring Mama had recovered and was able to attend church with us. We usually picked up Grandpa, as he couldn't walk to church anymore like he had for many years.

Graduation was May 24, which also happened to be Mama and Papa's 25th wedding anniversary. That day was a beautiful spring day. The birds woke us up with their singing, and we were all up early to get ready to go to church, as we usually did every Sunday. Mama asked Edith to make a couple of pies for our dinner when we returned from church. Edith was trying to make excuses why she didn't make the pies. She knew the neighbors had a surprise party planned for Mama and Papa's anniversary. Finally, we were ready to drive the ten miles to church. We were all in the car when Edith said suddenly, "I forgot something!" and ran back into the house. She was unhooking the lock on the door so the neighbors could get in.

While we were at church, they came into our house and prepared a meal and had everything ready for when we returned. Someone had made a beautiful two-layer cake with white frosting and pink roses on it. It sat on a beautiful glass pedestal.

Grandpa was ready and waiting on his porch when we stopped by to pick him up. Papa jumped out of the car and went to help him down the steps and into the car.

"Well, today is the big day," Grandpa said as he settled himself next to me on the seat. "How do you feel, Little Tyke?" he teased.

"Oh, Grandpa! I feel too old to be called Little Tyke. But just today it's okay, because all the people I love are together for my special day," I said.

"Well, it's another special day if I recall correctly," he said. "Happy Anniversary to you, John and Nellie. You are both looking quite dapper today. In fact, everyone is dressed so nicely you would think we were going to a funeral," he said with a laugh.

Grandpa was such a teaser and loved to make a joke with a punch line. Usually, he was the only one who got the punch line, but he would throw back his head and laugh and laugh. I knew he was teasing when his eyes had a twinkle that I loved so.

Edith seemed preoccupied that morning and was very unsettled in church. I looked at her and wondered what was going on. I asked her, "Why are you so fidgety today?" She just shrugged her shoulders and looked straight ahead.

Papa gave the sermon that day because our pastor was out of town. I loved seeing him up in the pulpit. He was so tall and commanding. He started out by saying, "Today many students at Canton High School will be graduating and going out into the world to make their own way. My daughter, Mary Ellen, is among them. Would the graduates please stand as we honor you?"

There were about ten of us that attended the Methodist church. We stood and everyone clapped for us. I felt like my heart was going to burst with pride. Having Papa, Mama, Aunt Mary, Edith, and Grandpa Sletten there made me feel warm all over, and I noticed that Mama had her hankie and was dabbing her eyes. I was especially happy that my Mama was sitting by my side.

As we sat back down and Papa started speaking, I noticed that he was trying to compose himself. Then he said, "We are so blessed to have my wife here with us. Twenty-five years ago today, she became my wife. That was one of the happiest days of my life. We are also blessed to have my father, Ingvold, with us today. God has blessed our family abundantly, and I thank Him for his watchful care over us. Let us pray."

After church everyone congregated on the front sidewalk to congratulate the graduates and wish Mama and Papa a happy anniversary. Edith seemed anxious for us to get going home and tried to steer Mama and Papa towards the car. "Edith," Mama finally said, "Why are you in such a hurry? You would think there was a fire someplace."

"I'm sorry, Mama, but today is going to be a big day, and I want you to be able to lay down and rest before the graduation tonight. That's all," she replied.

Soon we were on our way home and Grandpa said, "I think we should sing something while we're all together. How about singing "Praise God from Whom All Blessings Flow"?

Our voices raised together as we sang.

Praise God, from whom all blessing flow;
Praise Him all creatures here below;
Praise Him above, ye heavenly host;
Praise Father, Son, and Holy Ghost. A-men.[1]

---

1 Ken, Thomas. (1674). "Praise God, From Whom All Blessings Flow." Public domain: *https://hymnary.org/text/praise_god_from_whom_all_blessings_ken*

Our voices blended so well but mine was the usual monotone, which stuck out from all the rest.

"Let's sing another one, Papa," I said.

"Well, because it is a beautiful spring day and planting has begun, how about 'Bringing in the Sheaves?'" he said as he started us out.

Sowing in the morning, Sowing seeds of kindness,
Sowing in the noontide and the dewy eve;
Waiting for the harvest and the time of reaping,
We shall come rejoicing, Bringing in the sheaves.
Bringing in the sheaves, bringing in the sheaves,
We shall come rejoicing, Bringing in the sheaves.
Bringing in the sheaves, Bringing in the sheaves,
We shall come rejoicing, Bringing the sheaves.[2]

As we turned into our driveway, Papa exclaimed, "What are all these cars doing here? Was there a fire that everyone came to help with?"

Edith was the first one out of the car and ran into the house. Then people started coming out of the house and greeting us as we walked toward them. "Happy Anniversary!" they all called out together.

Mama and Papa were walking holding hands as they often did, and I was holding Grandpa's hand to steady him. We were all so surprised seeing all our neighbors there. Edith was the only one who wasn't surprised.

---

2 Shaw, Knowles. (1874). "Bringing in the Sheaves, Bringing in the Sheaves." Public domain: *https://hymnary.org/text/sowing_in_the_morning_sowing_seeds*

John and Nellie Sletten's 25th Wedding Anniversary Party
May 1936

"That's why I couldn't get you to make those pies this morning," Mama said to her.

"I had a hard time avoiding that, but I knew the neighbors were bringing everything, including desserts, to the party," she confessed.

We all went inside, and our neighbors had a wonderful meal prepared. When Mama saw the beautiful, two-tiered cake all decorated, she said, "It's just too beautiful to eat!" After the meal, Mama and Papa went outside, and someone took a picture of the happy couple with Mama holding the cake up proudly.

As I watched them, I thought to myself wistfully, *I wonder if someday I'll be standing next to my husband, with our children looking on, at our twenty-fifth wedding anniversary.*

Mama and Papa cut the cake, and we all had a big piece with homemade ice cream on top. It was delicious. Then good-byes were said and one by one the neighbors headed home.

When the house was quiet, Edith guided Mama to her room and made sure she rested before graduation that evening. Grandpa and Papa sat in the living room and visited, but soon their heads were laid back and they, too, were taking a nap.

I tried to lie down and nap also, but I was so excited that I couldn't even shut my eyes. The afternoon seemed to drag on. I didn't think the nappers would ever wake up so we could be on our way.

Finally, everyone was up, dressed, and in the car heading to Canton once more. I grew more excited as we neared the high school. I had attended the graduation services of other classes, but tonight it was my turn to walk across that big stage and receive my diploma. We all entered the large auditorium and Mama, Papa, Edith, and Grandpa found seats that Aunt Mary had saved for them.

I rushed to the room where my class was assembling. They were all talking and putting on their robes and mortarboards, making sure the tassels were on the right side. Ethel came up to me and gave me a big hug. "Can you believe it? We're graduating from high school. I will miss you so much, Mary Ellen. I have loved being your roommate these last four years."

"Oh, Ethel, we will always stay in touch, I promise," I said as we helped each other put our mortarboards on and made sure our hair looked just right. Then we all lined up and waited for the organ to begin playing "Pomp and Circumstance," the essential song for a graduation ceremony. Soon the music started and we filed down the aisle in pairs. When I passed my family, I felt a hand reach out and touch mine. I turned and my Papa was there, looking so proud of me. Mama was dabbing her eyes already, and Edith, Grandpa, and Aunt Mary were smiling widely.

I don't think I heard much of the graduation address. I was dreaming of what my life ahead would hold. Soon it was time for us to walk across that big stage and receive our diplomas. When it was my turn, I looked out to see where my family was sitting and they were all waving at me.

"Mary Ellen Sletten," the principal said my name. I walked across the stage with my heart beating rapidly and received my diploma. I moved my tassel to the left side and walked off the stage. As I moved my tassel, I thought how I was moving into another stage of my life, my adult stage. What would it bring? What exciting things will I experience? Then, I thanked God for bringing me to this point in my life and for giving me a wonderful family and many wonderful friends.

24

GOING TO COLLEGE

I DIDN'T KNOW HOW TO approach Papa about college. I knew we didn't have any extra money for me to go. Things were really bad in the state with the drought, some places worse than others. We were still able to feed our milk cows and we had the chickens, so we were still able to sell the milk, cream, butter, and eggs in town. Edith was still at home taking care of Mama, so there were four mouths to feed. I know Papa owed the doctor for all the calls he made to see Mama. I felt selfish to want to go off to college and leave Edith there alone to manage Mama and help Papa. But I wanted to go so I could make my own way and be able to help Mama and Papa financially. If I could get a good job as a teacher, I could have money to help them. I know Papa had always said that he wanted his girls to get a good education so they could make their own way.

But now things were different. One day I decided to walk out to the field Papa was plowing. It was just a stubble field, and nothing had been harvested from it. The corn field was dried up and the grasshoppers were busy eating what was left.

"Papa," I said timidly, "you have always said that you wanted Edith and me to have an education. Isn't that right?"

"Well, I have said that," he said as he stopped working, "and I still want that, but I don't know how long this drought is going to last. This year has been the hardest since it began. But I know you have your heart set on going to Dakota Wesleyan in Mitchell, and we will find a way for you to do that, at least for two years. That is what we did for Edith, and I think we can do it for you."

"Oh Papa," I said as I pushed the dry dirt around with my toe, "I am so excited to be able to go, and I will work really hard. I know I can find a job where I can earn some of my tuition."

"I've been thinking about things, and I think I may be able to get you a scholarship from the Methodist church, since I'm a lay preacher. That would really help you. I'll talk to the church board and see what they can offer," he said as we walked together in the stubble field.

That evening after we had done the milking, I looked at Papa and, suddenly, he looked old to me. He had worked so hard to make this farm what it is, and now he was uncertain what would happen to it. I decided I didn't mind separating the milk, so I told Papa to go in the house and I would do it myself. All I could think about as I ran the separator was how wonderful college was going to be. A whole new life was about to open up for me. What would the next few years bring? Two years in college and then I could get a job and be on my own, plus be able to help Papa. I could just see myself sitting at my desk where I worked, typing away happily, and then picking up my paycheck every Friday.

Two weeks later in mid-July, Papa went before the board of the Methodist church in Canton and asked for a scholarship for me to attend Dakota Wesleyan. I was on pins and needles waiting for him to get home that evening. Finally, I saw him pull into the driveway and I ran out to meet him.

"Papa, what did they say?" I asked as he had barely stopped in front of the house.

"They will give you a hundred dollars a year towards your tuition. And Mrs. Nelson said she has a sister who lives not far from the campus, and she always needs a girl to help her keep house and cook for her. Her name is Mrs. Pearson. She pays twenty-five cents an hour. I got her number, and you can call her tomorrow and apply for the job," Papa said as we walked to the barn to do the nightly milking.

I could hardly wait for tomorrow to come. Sleep didn't come easy that night.

After we finished milking the next morning, and I thought it was not too early, I called the number Papa had given me and talked to Mrs. Pearson. I liked her right away, and she was pleased with what I told her about myself. I would work on Saturday mornings for about two hours at twenty-five cents per hour.

"I got the job, Papa!" I exclaimed as he came into the kitchen. "I'm going to start packing my trunk right away!"

"Whoa there, Little Tyke, we have some fieldwork to do before you start packing," he said as he pulled on his hat and boots. "We still have hay to make today."

"Oh, I forgot," I said as I got my hat and gloves. Edith was there too, and she was about as excited for me as I was. We all headed out to the field and worked until noon, then headed into the house for dinner.

My going to college was the main topic at the dinner table that day. Edith said she would make me a couple of new dresses, and that I could have her Sunday shoes, as she could use her old shoes until she could get another pair for herself.

After lunch Papa said, "I think Edith and I can finish up out in the field this afternoon. Why don't you stay in the house with Mama, and she can help you start packing?"

"You don't have to tell me twice!" I said as I ran up the stairs and into the storage room over the kitchen to get the old trunk from under the eaves. I drug it up the two steps into the hall and down the hall to my room. It was so musty and smelled of moth balls, but I soon had it wiped out and sprayed with some of my perfume to take away the moth ball smell. It looked quite large for what little I had in my closet to take with me. But then I remembered I would have to bring bedding, pillows, and towels also. *It will be just right,* I said to myself. I put two blankets in the bottom, as I wouldn't need those this summer. Then I put some of my winter clothes and coat in, as I wouldn't need those before leaving either. It was filling up nicely.

Soon it was time to start supper for the family. Mama was up from her nap and peeling the potatoes when I entered the kitchen.

"I'm sorry I didn't help you with your packing, but I was just so tired, I thought I would take a little nap. When I woke up, I realized it was almost four. I guess I really needed that nap," she said as she put the potatoes on the stovetop.

Mary Ellen's high school senior picture, 1936

"Oh, that's okay, Mama," I said. "I really don't need to be in such a big hurry. It will still be about a month before I leave. How about if I make a nice pie to celebrate my going to college?"

"That will be great," Mama said. "I am so proud of you, Mary Ellen. You have grown up to be a wonderful young lady. My prayers have been answered, that I could see both my girls graduate from high school before I die."

"Mama, don't talk like that. I know you will be around for a long time and will live to see your grandchildren, of whom I plan on having quite a few for you," I said, trying to keep it lighthearted.

When I turned to look at her, I saw big tears running down her face. "Oh, Mary Ellen," she said through sobs, "I pray that will be the case, but I know that my days are numbered, and you will have to do without me very soon. I am so sorry that I haven't been a well mother for you growing up, and I have had to rely on you and Edith for taking care of so much around here."

We never were the type of family that hugged each other, but I went over and put my arms around her and gave her a big hug. "I love you, Mama. You have been a wonderful mother and have taught me so much growing up. I will miss you, but will write to you every week and let you know what I'm doing. Now, dry those tears, this is a happy time, not a sad time. We have supper to make."

The next few weeks went by in a flurry, and on the twenty-ninth of August, I was on the train in Canton heading to Mitchell, with Mama, Papa, and Edith standing on the station platform waving goodbye. My excitement turned to fear, and I was already homesick. I remembered when I had to stay in town for three weeks during the blizzard and how much I missed my family. We had already decided that I would stay in Mitchell over Thanksgiving due to the cost of train tickets. The sun was shining bright that day when the train pulled out of the station. My eyes blurred with tears as the miles passed. I was leaving home and starting on my own journey in life.

Papa had given me a five-dollar bill, and I knew in order to give it to me he would have to go without something. I was full of gratitude for my family and what they had done to get me to this point in my life, and I thanked God for giving them to me. *Help me, Lord, to do what is pleasing to You, and help me to make my family proud of me,* I whispered as I stared out the window, watching the miles go past while the train took me farther and farther from home and closer and closer to my new life as an adult.

Mr. and Mrs. Pearson were at the station to meet me and take me to the college. Right away I knew I liked them, and I was happy that I had a job. They drove past their beautiful house on the way to the college. It was one of the most beautiful houses I had ever seen. I couldn't believe that I was going to work there.

When we pulled up to the girl's dorm, there were girls sitting out front on the steps talking. I suddenly felt very self-conscious. *Do I have the right clothes? Am I smart enough to get good grades?* It was just like the first day of high school, except much worse. Mr. Pearson carried my trunk up the stairs to the second floor, and Mrs. Pearson helped me find my room. "Here it is, Mary Ellen, number 211. This will be your new home for the next two years.

There was a pretty young girl sitting on one of the beds. "Hello," she said as she stood to greet us. She was tall and had long dark hair, which she had pulled up in a bun. "My name is Sharon Bethel, and you must be Mary Ellen."

I put my hand out to shake hers. "Yes, that's my name and it is nice to meet you." Then I had nothing else to say, but she started showing me what drawers were mine and where I could hang my dresses. She was easy to talk to and I felt comfortable being with her.

After Mrs. and Mr. Pearson left, and I had put all my things away, we sat on our beds and talked. Before I knew, it was time to go to supper. Sharon was from Rapid City and grew up on a ranch near there. We found we had a lot in common. She also had only one older brother, and because her family had milk cows, she knew all about milking chores.

Sharon had arrived the night before, so she had already looked over the campus. After supper she gave me a guided tour. It was so big, with several large buildings in which I would have to find my classes. The next day we would register for what classes we wanted to take.

As we walked back to our dorm, Sharon said, "We can look at what classes we want to take tonight, so when we go to register, we'll know just what we want, and then we can find the building where they're held. That way, on the first day of class, we'll know exactly where to go."

I was glad that I had Sharon for my roommate. She and I would get along just great. It was strange going to sleep in a different bed in a dorm full of other girls with a girl I just met sleeping in a bed on the other side of the room. I said my prayers and thanked God for leading me and watching over me, even selecting my roommate. God knew just what I needed.

HOME FOR CHRISTMAS

WOW! COLLEGE WAS so different from high school. My high school typing teacher was so supportive and really boosted my confidence. My college teacher was just the opposite. I felt I couldn't please her no matter what I did. My roommate told me that some college professors try to weed people out by being tough on them. That's all I needed to hear. I just became more determined. I would keep working hard, but that was not my priority—having fun was.

I never knew college could be so much fun. The dormitory girls got together to play Rook or dominoes, or we just sat around and gabbed until it was lights out, which was nine o'clock. One of our favorite topics was boys.

One Saturday night we were playing Rook when Sharon said, "Mary Ellen, I think Roger White likes you. I see him looking at you in English class. I think he is just too shy to come and talk to you. You should talk to him sometime."

I looked up startled and said, "Why do you think I have enough courage to go up to him and start a conversation? I'm just as shy as he is—until I get to know someone—then you can hardly get a word in edgewise."

Roger was a nice-looking boy with blond hair. His build was a little stocky, and he was about five inches taller than me. He was in a couple of my classes, and I hadn't really noticed him much. I decided that I wanted to get my teaching degree before I got serious with anyone and maybe have a couple of years teaching under my belt before even thinking about marriage. Maybe if the right time presented itself, I would talk to him sometime. For now, I was going to put Roger White out of my mind.

I loved working for Mrs. Pearson. She had many fancy dinner parties, and she taught me a lot about how to set the table and serve the meal to her guests. She also showed me how to make fancy deserts and salads. I worked every Saturday morning cleaning and getting the house ready for her company that evening.

One Saturday after I finished the cleaning and polished the silver set, Mrs. Pearson came in the kitchen with a box full of clothes and said, "I thought you might be able to wear some of my daughter's old dresses. They are perfectly good, and I think you are about her size. Take them into the spare bedroom and try them on. You can have whatever you like."

I could hardly believe my eyes when I opened the box and started taking out dress after dress. They were beautiful, and there were also some slips and undergarments. I was shaking as I tried on each dress. There were a couple that were just too fancy for me, but most of them were just what I would have picked out at the store, and they fit me perfectly. I would probably have to hem most of them as Mrs. Pearson's daughter was a little taller than I was. I could hardly wait to get back to the dorm and show them to Sharon.

When I came back down the curved staircase, I had on one of the new dresses. I felt so elegant and went to find Mrs. Pearson to thank her.

She was still in the kitchen having a cup of tea. "Mrs. Pearson, how can I thank you for all these clothes? I feel like it is too much," I said as I twirled around in the new dress I was going to wear back to my dorm. "Most of them fit me just perfectly. I left the formal ones, as I'm not sure I will have a use for them."

"Why, Mary Ellen, that dress looks wonderful on you," she said as she stood to look at me closely. "I'm so happy you like them. I didn't want to have them hanging in the closet gathering dust."

I thanked her again, gathered my coat, and headed out the door with the cherished box. It was getting cold outside, and I was missing my family so much. I thought about what Edith and Mama would be making for Thanksgiving, which was coming up in a couple weeks. I guessed I'd be eating in the cafeteria by myself as Sharon was going home for Thanksgiving.

Sharon ooo'd and ahhh'd when she saw the dresses and other things. "Wow! You're sure lucky to be working at a rich person's house and to get such wonderful hand-me-downs."

"I will need you to help me pin a couple of them up since they're a little too long for me," I said as I hung the new dresses up in my closet.

The next Saturday Mrs. Pearson asked me if I was going home for Thanksgiving.

"No," I said, "it's too expensive to take the train home for Thanksgiving. I'm waiting until Christmas vacation. I am missing my family so much, but it was a stretch for them to even send me to college."

"Well, why don't you come and spend Thanksgiving Day with our family? Our daughters will be home, and we would love to have you join us," Mrs. Pearson said.

"That's so nice of you. I would love to spend the day with your family. It will help me not feel so homesick," I said. "I plan on calling them so at least I can hear their voices. My sister said Mama's not doing too well again, and they've had to hire a professional nurse to come in and take care of her. Plus, my Grandpa is failing also. My sister has been spending more time with him to help with housekeeping and taking care of him. I don't think I could ever be the one to take care of the elderly, but she seems to know just what to do."

Thanksgiving Day was wonderful. Mrs. Pearson's daughters were so nice, and they had more clothes they weren't wearing and were leaving at home. I went back to the dorm with a box full of clothes and a full stomach.

When I opened the box in my room, I could hardly believe what I found. Right on top was a beautiful, blue winter coat with fur on the collar. I almost cried it was so beautiful. I took it out and slipped it on. It fit perfectly and I looked so elegant in it. It was a little long, but it would be just right for the cold winter nights. I could hardly wait for Christmas break so I could wear it on the train ride home. I wouldn't wear it until then so I could keep it clean.

That night I hung the new coat on the closet door so I could look at it before I went to sleep, and so it would be the first thing I saw when I woke up in the morning. In my prayers that night, I thanked God for the clothes and the beautiful coat, which was my favorite color—blue.

Finally, it was Christmas break, and I would be heading home on the morning train to spend two whole weeks at home. I could hardly wait until morning. Sharon was taking a train in the opposite direction, so Mr. Pearson took us to the train station in the morning.

It was the first time I had worn my new blue coat. I couldn't wait to see my family and especially for them to see how much I had grown up. No one better call me Little Tyke anymore! I was a college woman. But deep down inside, I still felt like that little girl, just dressing up in women's clothing.

The train ride to Canton seemed to take forever, but soon the conductor announced, "Canton." I searched out the window for my family but didn't see anyone. *Surely they hadn't forgotten the date to pick me up,* I thought. As I was walking down the aisle towards the door, I saw Papa, standing there on the platform looking for me. My heart did a flip-flop. "Papa!" I called out, "Here I am, Papa!"

When he saw me, he looked a little confused but waved back. "Papa," I said as I rushed up to him and gave him a big hug. "I'm home. I can't believe I'm really home."

"Mary Ellen, I almost didn't recognize you. You have grown into a lovely lady. We have missed you so much, and I know Mama and Edith will think the same thing when they see you. They're waiting in the car, so let's get your bag and head home," Papa said as we walked to claim my bag.

When we got to the car, Papa put my bag in the trunk, and I climbed in the back seat with Edith and gave her a great big hug.

"Edith, I have missed you so much! And Mama, I am so happy to be home with all of you," I said as I put my hand on Mama's shoulder.

Of course, Mama was crying, but they were tears of happiness. "Mary Ellen, I almost didn't recognize you. Where did you get that lovely coat?" she asked as she dabbed her eyes.

"Mrs. Pearson's daughters have given me many new clothes that they don't wear anymore, and I got this beautiful coat at Thanksgiving when I spent the day with them," I replied.

"It's beautiful, Mary Ellen, and it makes your blue eyes all the bluer," Edith said as she stroked the fur on the collar.

"Edith, I brought a couple of the dresses for you that I didn't want to hem. I think they will fit you perfectly," I said as we pulled out of the train station and headed west out of Canton.

I could hardly wait to be home and in my own bed. "How's Grandpa?" I asked Edith.

"Well, he is doing a little better. That's why I'm coming home today, since he feels like he can manage for a few days. It's hard to see him get weaker and frailer, but he still has his sense of humor and wit," Edith said as we pulled into the driveway.

The house looked the same, but it somehow looked much smaller than I remembered. The barn was there, and the cows in the barnyard turned their heads to look at us as we drove past. "Where's Tiger?" I asked. "She usually comes running when we get home."

Papa answered, "I'm sorry, Tiger died a few days ago. I noticed she didn't come into the barn at milking time a couple of days in a row, so I went up in the hayloft and found her. She looked like she was just sleeping peacefully. I left her there, as her body was frozen, and I can't bury her until the ground thaws a little. I thought you would like to say goodbye to her, Mary Ellen, since she's been your cat since you were eight years old. I'll go with you."

Papa and I went to the barn, while Mama and Edith went into the house. As I approached Tiger lying in the hay, she didn't even look like Tiger, but she looked peaceful as if she had just lain down in the hay and died.

"Goodbye, Tiger," I said while I stroked her fur. "You have been such a good kitty for so many years. I'll miss you," I said as I wiped a tear from my eye.

Papa and I walked slowly back to the house without saying a word. Papa knew how much I loved Tiger, and there was nothing he could say to take away that hurt. When we entered the kitchen, there was a wonderful aroma of apple pies that Edith had made, and Mama had put a roast with potatoes and carrots in the oven for a special coming home meal. I took my bag upstairs and carefully hung my new coat in the closet. It was so good to be home. I just stood there and soaked in all the sights and smells of home.

The next day was Christmas, and Aunt Mary had invited us to join her, Uncle Charlie, and Grandpa at the diner in town. What a special meal we had. It was so good to see her and Uncle Charlie and Grandpa. Grandpa needed help getting to his place at the table, but he still had that twinkle in his eye.

"How's my Little…," he stopped and gave me a wink, "my little Mary Ellen? You look beautiful in that blue coat. It makes you look so grown up, and you have turned into a very lovely young lady." I gave him a hug. "Thanks, Grandpa, I sure have missed you and our Rook games. We play it at college all the time, but it's not the same as playing with you," I told him.

After our meal we all went over to Grandpa's house and had such a wonderful visit. We talked about the time we all went to the cemetery in Parker last Memorial Day. I remembered Grandpa went to each of his childrens' graves. First, to Anthony's grave on the end of the row with the First World War marker. Next, to Thomas, Amil, and little Peter and said a prayer. Then, he went to Grandma Sletten's grave and knelt down, which was hard for him. He placed his hand on her grave and traced her name with his finger. There were tears running down his face. "I'll be seeing you soon, Belle," he said and then asked Papa to help him up from his knees.

Papa then helped him walk to his brother Ole's grave, who had died just five years before. His sister, Caroline, had died in 1925, about ten years ago, and was buried in Wisconsin. Brother Samuel died suddenly the same year. I remember that it was quite a shock to the family. He was buried in the Worthing Cemetery. His brothers—Martin, Edward, and Thomas—were all still living, as was his youngest sister, Alena.

I remember thinking that someday this generation will be gone. I was thankful for all they had taught us about living life, and the legacy they would leave us when they were gone.

Soon it was time to head back to the farm. Edith was staying with Grandpa, as Mama was doing better, and I would be home for a couple of weeks to help take care of her. I took her arm as we walked down the sidewalk to the car. She was my Mama, but right now I felt like she was my child while I watched so she didn't slip on the icy spots.

Back home, after Papa and I did the milking, we all sat around the dining room table and visited about the past. We had roast beef sandwiches and finished up the pie. *This will be a Christmas I will never forget,* I thought. I soaked it all in until my heart was so full, I thought it might burst. "Thank you, God, for giving me my family," I said to myself. Then I settled back in my chair and listened to Papa and Mama recalling old times.

26

GOODBYE, GRANDPA

CHRISTMAS VACATION WENT BY much too fast, and soon I was on the train heading back to DWU. I would miss my family. One thing I wouldn't miss was the outhouse! I was happy to be getting back to the dorm with bathrooms and showers which I had gotten used to.

This was a new semester, and I started it with a new goal—to be the best teacher I could be. I was taking more secretarial classes along with the usual required classes. One that I really enjoyed was speech. I found that I loved writing and giving speeches. I had always been so shy and never wanted to get up in front of a group to talk, but I really took a liking to it. It gave me so much poise and confidence. I also had more confidence when it came to talking to people I didn't know. I became much more outgoing, which I liked about myself. I was always an outgoing person, but much more reserved and shy until I really got to know people.

One day I was walking to class when I saw Roger White, so I stopped and said, "Hi, Roger, what class are you going to?"

Roger just about turned and ran when I talked to him but regained his composure and answered, "Chemistry." A redness moved across his face and ears like I had never seen before.

"How about if we walk together? I'm going that way too. Sure is a nice day for February. You would almost think it was spring, but we know better than that in South Dakota," I said trying to put him at ease.

"It sure is, but we can get some nice days in February. Say, Mary Ellen, I—I was wondering if you would like to go to the, uh, Valentine's Stroll with me," he blurted out as his face turned a new color of red.

I had heard about the "stroll," which was the Methodist's way of having a social gathering for students since dancing was not allowed. Music was played, and the couples could walk, hand in hand if they wished, around the gym floor. It sounded kind of fun, and this would be my first official date. "Sure," I said. "I would like that."

Roger's eyes got wide and he swallowed, making his Adam's apple move up and down. "Okay, so I'll pick you up at your dorm at seven that night," he said as he hurried off to his chemistry class.

I watched him as he sped away and thought, Nope, he's not the one, but he's a nice guy. It would be fun to have a date to the stroll. I wondered if he would want to hold my hand. Then I thought, What will I wear? I was happy that I had the dresses from Mrs. Pearson, because I knew just the one I would wear. It was white with red trim and flowers on the cuffs. It wasn't really a winter dress, so I had been saving it for spring. It would make a great Valentine's dress. Now I was getting excited. I had a hard time focusing on my shorthand class, but soon class was over and I was heading back to the dorm. I couldn't wait to tell Sharon about my date.

"Guess what?" I blurted out as I entered our room. I didn't wait for her to answer me, "I have a date to the Valentine's Stroll! Can you believe it?"

Sharon stood and we both jumped up and down with excitement. "Who are you going with?" Sharon asked.

"You will never believe it. Today when I was walking to short-hand class, I came across Roger White," I said. "I stopped him and actually had enough courage to talk to him. He was going to chemistry class. I figured he was that kind of guy, a real brain. Anyway, I just chit-chatted about the weather, and he acted like he was going to bolt, but he responded to me. His face was the color of a tomato, and every time he swallowed, his Adam's apple bobbed up and down. I had a hard time concentrating because I was so intrigued by his Adam's apple moving. I've never seen one that stuck out so much. Anyway, he came right out and asked me if I wanted to go to the stroll with him. I said sure, and he took off for class. I guess he is like me; he's probably never been on a date in his whole life." I began to pull dresses out of the closet. "Here's the one I think I will wear," I said as I pulled out the white and red one.

"That one is perfect for a Valentine's dance," Sharon said.

"It's not a dance. My Papa would come get me and take me right home if he found out I went to a dance. It's called a stroll," I said with confidence.

"Oh yah, I have heard about that. Sounds like it's fun, and you can talk and get to know each other. Maybe even hold hands," she said with a sigh and a dreamy look in her eyes.

The day of the stroll seemed to take forever to arrive. I had talked a few times with Roger, and he even sat with me for lunch one day. We didn't have a lot in common, but he was a nice enough fella and once he got over being so shy, we had a good conversation.

"What color dress will you be wearing?" he asked while we ate our lunch.

I wasn't sure why he wanted to know that, but I told him it was white and red with colored flowers around the cuffs.

"Good," he replied, "that way most any color of flowers will go with it. What color flowers do you like?"

"Oh, I really like roses, and I like pink the best," I said, even though I had never had flowers from a boy before, and even a dandelion corsage would have been welcomed. I thought to myself, *Wow, he's really doing it up right. Even getting me a corsage. I wonder if I need to get him a boutonniere? I'll ask Mrs. Pearson; she'll know what the etiquette is for that.*

The day finally arrived, and I was dressed and waiting in the dorm lobby with boutonniere in hand for Roger. I felt like a princess in my new dress, and I even had some nice white shoes I got from Mrs. Pearson's daughters. All the other girls who were going to the stroll were waiting in the lobby. Such beautiful dresses, but I didn't feel like mine was any less pretty, even though it was a hand-me-down.

One by one the girls left with their dates until I was the only one left sitting in the lobby. *What could have happened to Roger? Did he get cold feet?* Finally, I saw him coming up the walk toward the dorm. He looked really nice in his dark suit, and he had a box in his hand.

I let him in, and he apologized for being late. He said he realized at the last minute his shoes needed polishing which slowed him down. He took the corsage out of the box, and with shaking hands, pinned it to my dress. It was made of beautiful pink roses with a pink ribbon. I pinned his boutonniere on his jacket lapel, and we were off. It was only a short distance to the gym, and we walked in silence. I guess neither one of us had much to say at that point.

I heard the music coming from the gym as we approached. "Do you like this music?" I asked as we entered the gym.

"Oh, it's okay. I like waltzes," he said.

We started strolling around, and I couldn't think of a thing to talk about. Then I suddenly thought of asking him about his family. That's always a good conversation starter.

"How many kids are in your family? I only have one sister," I said.

"We have a pretty big family," he responded. "There are six of us. Four boys and two girls. I'm the youngest in the family."

He was swallowing again, and I couldn't help but look at his Adam's apple. From the side, it really stuck out. Almost more than his nose! We walked along making small talk, and soon we were more comfortable with each other. About halfway through the night, Roger reached down and took my hand and asked, "I hope you don't mind if I hold your hand while we walk."

"Oh no," I said. "Hold away." As soon as the words came out of my mouth I thought, *Why did I say that? What came over me?* He laughed, so I laughed. I remember thinking what a great laugh he had. We enjoyed the rest of the evening walking together and holding hands, except when he went to get us refreshments.

He walked me back to the dorm and said goodnight. "Maybe we can 'stroll away' another time, just around campus," he said, teasing me about my saying, "Hold away."

"I would like that," I replied with enthusiasm. "Anytime would be great. Good night, Roger," I said as he turned and walked down the sidewalk toward his dorm.

Sharon was waiting up for me to hear all about my date. We talked until lights out and more after that until the house mother came and told us to shush and get to sleep. It was a great night, and I had a hard time getting to sleep for thinking about my night with Roger.

Three days later while I was in my dorm room studying, the dorm mother came to our room and said I had a telephone call. That was unusual, as Papa and Mama only called me on Sundays and today was Tuesday. *I hope Mama is okay,* I thought as I walked down to the lobby, picked up the receiver, and said, "Hello."

"Mary Ellen." It was Papa on the other end. "I have some bad news for you tonight," he said. "Grandpa went into the hospital today, and he passed away this afternoon. The doctor said he had developed pneumonia and just couldn't fight it. He really didn't suffer at all, but just kind of drifted off to sleep and didn't wake up."

There was silence on the line until I finally said, "Oh no, I knew it would happen sometime, but I really wanted to be there to tell him goodbye." My throat felt tight, and my eyes filled with tears. "I just can't believe my Grandpa is gone."

Papa told me that the funeral would be on Saturday, and that I could take the train home on Friday. He had arranged for my ticket.

"Papa," I said, "it must be really hard to lose your dad. That's something I don't want to know about." I said goodbye and hung the receiver back on its cradle.

It didn't seem real. Grandpa would never come out to the farm for Sunday dinner ever again. I would never, ever be able to sit next to him in the pew at church. He would never again show me how he could put his leg behind his head while he sat on the floor—something he could still do up until about a year ago. My Grandpa was gone. It just seemed like a bad dream.

Friday morning Mr. Pearson took me to the train station, and I was on my way home. It was not a happy trip, like when I went home for Christmas. I thought to myself as the train pulled out of the station, *I wonder what Grandpa will look like dead?* I couldn't picture it. He was always so full of life and had a way about him that made everything seem okay. The way he told stories and the way he threw his head back and laughed. I would miss that so much. Life would be a little emptier without Grandpa.

Saturday morning, we were all sitting in our church pew, but Grandpa was up front in a casket. *He should be sitting here with us,* I thought. Papa looked so sad as he had to say goodbye to his dad. Mama had handed out hankies to all of us if we needed them. We did. Edith reached out and took my hand and squeezed it. We cried softly together.

When the funeral was over, I had to go back to school. Papa dropped me off at the station and they headed to Parker where Grandpa would be buried with his children and Grandma.

When the train came to the railroad crossing over the road to Parker, I saw Papa, Mama, and Edith standing by the road waving to me. I waved back…and then they were gone. It finally hit me; my Grandpa was gone.

SUMMER VACATION

A s i excitedly packed my little trunk to go home for the summer, I thought about the many good memories of my first year of college. I loved college life, and I was looking forward to the fall and to my second and last year. But it would feel good to get back home and outside helping Papa with the fieldwork and the milking. I never thought I would miss those chores, but it was part of "home." I said goodbye to Sharon at the train station, as she was leaving on a different train going west.

Last night I said goodbye to Roger. He had decided to transfer to the School of Mines in Rapid City. I knew he would do great things with his life, and I wished him well. As I walked back to my dorm, I thought, *Well, I didn't find Mr. Right this year...maybe next year. What did Lucy used to tell me in high school? There are plenty of fish in the sea.* She was right. I had plenty of time to find Mr. Right. After all, I was only nineteen, soon to be twenty. Boy, when I said it that way, I realized I wouldn't be a teen anymore. Twenty did seem old!

When I arrived back in Canton, Papa was there to greet me. It was good to see him, but he looked older somehow. His shoulders seemed to sag, and his step was not quite as quick as it was. He looked tired and worn out.

"Papa," I asked. "How is Mama doing?"

"Well, she isn't doing very well," he said. "She has been having small strokes and just isn't herself anymore. I'm grateful to have Edith home with us. She is such a help with Mama. I don't know what I would do without her. We hired a professional nurse to take care of Mama a few times, but that gets quite expensive. It will be good to have you home with us, Mary Ellen. We have missed you, and I can sure use the help with the fieldwork and cows."

"Oh, Papa," I said as I took his arm, "maybe I should stay home this next year to help you and Edith. I can always go back the year after that." My heart hurt to think about not going back to college, but I knew Papa would not ask me to stay home.

"No, Mary Ellen, Mama and I want you to finish your education. We can manage with Edith home now. After all, in the winter there isn't much to do except milk the cows and take care of the chickens. Edith and I are managing that. I'm sure she'll be glad to have your help over the summer," he said as he loaded my trunk into the car.

Soon we were on the familiar road home. Papa let me drive from the five-mile corner to our place, and he even let me drive down the driveway. I loved driving and could hardly wait to get my own car someday.

Edith came out of the house to greet us. "Mary Ellen, I'm so happy to have you home again. It just doesn't seem like home without you here. Come in, I have dinner all ready."

The sights and smells of home hit me as I entered the back door. Edith was such a good cook and had a wonderful meal ready for us. Mama was up and happy to see me, but she looked as if she didn't know me.

"Mama, it's Mary Ellen," I said as I gave her a big hug.

"Oh, my little Mary Ellen is home," she said. "Where have you been today?"

I knew I had to play along with her, so I just said, "I've been at school, Mama. I'm learning how to become a teacher."

"Oh, that's nice," she said as Edith helped her out of her rocking chair and guided her to the dining room table.

Here we all were, sitting in the cheerful dining room with the sun shining though the stained glass around the big south window. Papa said the prayer, and I echoed it in my mind. *Yes, thank you, God, for my family and especially that my Mama is still here with us.*

It was a busy summer, but soon I was back at the dorm and Sharon was there to greet me. We hugged and talked about our summers at home for a couple of hours.

This would be my last year there, and next spring I would graduate with a two-year teaching degree. I was excited to get my degree and be out on my own, but sad that I would be leaving this place that I called home now. Sharon was going to stay two more years so she could get a bachelor's degree.

I didn't see how I could possibly ask Papa to let me stay two more years. I had planned to get a job in Canton when I graduated so I would be close to him and Mama. I guess I would just have to think about it. In the meantime, I was going to have fun!

I got my job back with Mrs. Pearson, and she told me I was the best housekeeper she ever had. She also told me if I decided to stay in school another two years, she would be happy to have me stay on with her.

My classes were more difficult, but I soon learned how to study, which helped. There were several more boys I went on dates with, but none of them were right for me. Sharon had a steady boyfriend, so I went with her a couple times on a double date. We went to the five-cent movie and had pizza after. We had a lot of fun together.

When I was home for Christmas, I decided to ask Papa about staying in school another two years. We were sitting around the dining room table with our little Christmas tree in the center. I thought, *Now's as good a time as any.*

"Papa," I said, "I think I want to enroll in the four-year degree program at DWU. With only two more years, I will have a bachelor's degree and I can get better teaching jobs. I'll be able to earn more that way, and I can find a job anyplace. Aunt Mary said teachers are in high demand right now. She thinks it's a good idea.… What do you think?"

Papa was silent for some time and then he finally said, "I think that's an excellent idea, Mary Ellen. You will make a good teacher. You'd be following in Mama's and my footsteps. I think you can get more scholarship money from the Methodist church."

"Mrs. Pearson offered me my job back, so I'll be working to help pay for it," I said. I was so excited, I jumped up and gave Papa a big hug and kiss. "I will make you proud, Papa. I know I will."

That year passed quickly, and soon I was home for the summer again before I started my last two years at college. I worked hard with Papa and helped Edith with the housework and with Mama. Mama had never fully recovered from the stroke she had the year Grandpa died. She needed complete care and was in bed most of the time. I was sure when I left for college that fall, I wouldn't see her alive again, so I spent as much time with her as possible. We remembered how things were when I was little. She seemed to recall those stories, but she didn't remember things that had happened recently, that I was in college, or that I was going another two years to become a teacher. It was going to be hard to leave in September, but Papa said I shouldn't feel bad about going, as he and Mama wanted me to complete my degree.

July 20, 1938, my twentieth birthday, was a wonderful birthday for me. Papa teased me about being twenty and not even a prospect for a husband on the horizon. "Oh, Papa," I said, "there are a lot of eligible boys at college. I just need to find the right one. You just wait, I bet by this time next year, I will have found Mr. Right."

I had my old high school friends over for dinner, and we all played croquet in the afternoon. We had such a good time reminiscing about our high school days. Papa had brought Mama's rocker out on the front porch so she could watch us play. She seemed to enjoy being outside and loved watching us. Croquet was one of her favorite games.

That night Mama was very tired, and Edith put her to bed early. Papa, Edith, and I sat up talking until late in the evening when Papa said, "Time to turn in," as he turned the kerosine lamp down.

Next month I would be going back to DWU for my junior year. I was excited, but worried about Papa and Edith having to take on the whole load of the farm and Mama's care. I was torn between wanting to get my bachelor's degree and staying home to help on the farm. Something seemed to be telling me that everything would be okay and that I should go back to school. I slept well that night, and in the morning, I had a renewed feeling that I was doing the right thing.

28

HELLO, MR. RIGHT

T AKING THE TRAIN BACK to Mitchell was now old hat for me. I remembered the first time I left home two years ago and how scared and sad I was. I would miss my family terribly and wondered what experiences I would have in college. It had been my home for the last two years and would be my home for the next two years, barring anything happening. I wondered what exciting things would happen to me and who I might meet that could change my life forever. Maybe Mr. Right.

As we pulled into the Mitchell train station, I spotted Mr. and Mrs. Pearson standing on the platform. I waved out the window at them. Now my stomach had butterflies because of the excitement of a new year at school. I could hardly wait to get to the dorm and see Sharon again. We had become close friends, and she was so happy that I was taking the four-year teaching program.

Soon we were pulling up to the front of the dorm. I scanned the girls outside sitting in the sun but didn't see Sharon. *She must be in our room unpacking,* I thought.

Mr. Pearson carried my trunk to my room for me. This year I was on the first floor, and he was happy about that. "There you go, Mary Ellen," he said as he set my trunk down. "We will see you on Saturday."

"Okay, Mr. Pearson. Thank you for picking me up today," I said as he left the room.

Sharon was not in the room, but her things were neat and in place. She was a very tidy person, unlike me. I tended to throw my clothes on the chair when I undressed and that drove her crazy.

"Mary Ellen, it doesn't take any more time to hang that dress up as throwing it on the chair. That way, it won't need pressing the next time you wear it," she'd tell me.

I busied myself putting my things in the drawers and hanging my dresses in the closet. I made up my bed and was going out the door to find Sharon when we collided in the doorway.

"Sharon, there you are!" I said. We both laughed and hugged each other. It was so good to be back at school and see Sharon again.

We sat on our beds and talked about our summers and what we had done. I told her about my Mama not doing very well. "I'm afraid I may not get to see her alive again," I said. "She's failing so fast. It about broke my heart to leave her, but Papa assured me they'd be fine, and Mama would want me to go back to school to get my teaching degree. Even though Mama couldn't understand everything I told her, she seemed to know I was getting an education and would be a teacher soon. She once told me that all she wanted was to live long enough to see her girls graduate from high school and go to college. I guess she's gotten her wish, but I pray she will be in my life for many more years. I want her to meet my Mr. Right."

"Do you have someone in mind for your Mr. Right?" Sharon asked.

"No, but I think this year is the year I will find him. Maybe someone new to college," I said as I looked wistfully out the window.

I was taking more secretarial classes, as well as classes on teaching. I really liked the aspects of learning how to teach a classroom full of students. It made me feel so grown up and in control. I had to take other classes, such as psychology, which I really enjoyed. I like to try to figure people out—find out what makes them tick—so psychology was right up my alley. Sharon was in that class also, and we had some good times in the dorm trying to analyze everyone.

I kept my eye out for Mr. Right—on my way to classes, in my classes, in the dining hall, and at worship, which we attended every morning. Sharon said she would keep her eye out also. "Four eyes are better than two," she said.

But I also really buckled down to get good grades. I had learned the last two years how to study, and I was proud of the grades I had finished with last year. I was out to get even better grades this year. But that didn't stop me from keeping an eye out for Mr. Right. I knew the minute I saw him I would know he was the one.

One evening Sharon and I were walking back to the dorm after attending a music program when we met several young men on the path. They stopped and talked to us for a few minutes, asking us where we were from and what we were taking in college.

They were very courteous and seemed very friendly. One of them was quite tall, about six feet at least, and he was about the most handsome man I had ever met. He had dark hair and seemed to take a liking to me. He was what we girls would call "tall, dark, and handsome." As we left them and walked on, I turned around and the tall one looked back at the same time and gave me a little wave. "Sharon!" I said. "That's him!"

"What do you mean?" she asked.

"I think I just met my Mr. Right," I said. I could hardly control myself for thinking about him. "You know, I was so engrossed in looking at him that I didn't catch his name. Did you?"

"I think he said Clark—it made me think of Clark, South Dakota. That would be a good way to remember it. He sure is a looker," she said.

"And very nice and soft spoken; I liked that. I hope we meet again soon," I told her as we went to our room and got ready for bed.

That night I couldn't sleep for thinking about Clark—Mr. Right. I had never had this feeling about anyone before. The thought of him made my heat beat faster and I had a warm feeling all over. Then I remembered it was kind of dark on the path when we met. Maybe when I see him in full light, he won't look as handsome. I didn't want to think about that. It would be terrible to see him the next time and find out he had bad teeth or a poor complexion and realize that Mr. Right was Mr. Wrong.

I didn't have to wait long. The next day I was sitting at a table eating supper when that tall, handsome boy came to the table and asked if he could sit with me. When I looked up, I saw he had wonderful teeth and a nice complexion. He was even more hand-some than he had been the night before. I suddenly became quite self-conscious and didn't know what to say. Finally, I said, "Sure, that would be great!"

He was easy to talk to, and I found out that he was a freshman and had a basketball scholarship. I just knew he was a basketball player, due to his height. I didn't know a lot about basketball, but I had a feeling I would learn a lot about it in the coming months.

The next Sunday Sharon and I were walking to church when we noticed two boys walking on the other side of the street. One of them was Clark. I didn't think they saw us, but when we sat down in church, they were right beside us. That day we ate together and then took a long walk downtown and ended up in East Side Park after getting lost trying to take a new way back to campus.

It was a wonderful day, and from then on, I was sure I had found Mr. Right. That night I sat down and wrote a letter to Papa.

Dear Papa,

I have found the man I think I will marry. He is a very nice Christian man. I know you will like him, and I know Mama will like him too. He is a freshman, but is only seven months younger than me, and has a basketball scholarship. I guess I will be going to many basketball games this year. He is from Frankfort, South Dakota, and has a large family—six sisters and two brothers. I still have a lot to learn about him, but so far, I like what I see. I'm looking forward to seeing you at Christmas. Have a good Thanksgiving and give Mama a kiss for me.

Love, Mary Ellen

P.S.: You can tell Edith about Clark. I guess I forgot to tell you his name. It's Clark Baird.

H. Clark Baird, picture given to Mary Ellen in 1938.
'From a pal to a great gal' written on the back.

29

GETTING ACQUAINTED

ONE SUPPER TOGETHER TURNED into every meal, every day. We sat at our usual table at the same time each meal and talked as we ate. As it turned out, Clark was working at the cafeteria, so he was able to meet up when it was convenient for me. He had all kinds of stories about working with Mrs. Moore, who was the cook. She was a jolly, buxom lady, and she could cook like no one else.

"Mrs. Moore is a machine," Clark told me one day. "She works for hours and never takes a break. She has me peeling potatoes, mixing up cake batter, and doing dishes all morning. Good thing I have classes in the afternoon, or she would keep me going all day. Oh, Mary Ellen," he continued, "I was so embarrassed today. She had her arms elbow deep in mixing up meat loaf when she suddenly said, 'Clark, come over here.' I went to her side, and she proceeded to instruct me as to what she wanted me to do. She said, 'Reach in under my blouse and pull up my bra strap. It's slipped down and is driving me crazy." I didn't know what to say or do, but when she tells you to do something, you do it, no questions asked. So, I gingerly slid my hand into her blouse and grabbed her very hefty bra strap and pulled it up on her shoulder. She thanked me profusely and went on with her mixing."

We laughed and laughed about that story while we ate, and laughed about it many times after that. Clark said it was because he had so many sisters that he even knew anything about bra straps.

Every Sunday Clark picked me up and we walked to church together. We both had strong faith and believed that being part of a church was important. He was also a Methodist, so that made me happy. There was so much more I wanted to know about Clark, his family, and his growing up years. Of course, I told him about my family and how things had been the last few years with the drought.

One particular Sunday after we ate together, we decided to walk downtown to get a "Big Deal" double dip ice cream cone. That was what we did for a date, but I didn't mind, as long as I was walking next to Clark. We sat at a small table in the ice cream parlor and talked.

"You need to tell me more about yourself," I said as I licked the cherry, nut ice cream cone. "Tell me about your mom and dad, brothers, sisters, and what kind of things you did when you were growing up."

I knew he lived near Frankfort on a farm and that it was close to Redfield. He laughed when I told him what my Papa had said when red dirt blew into our farm, that it "must have blown clear from Redfield." I loved his laugh. He would throw back his head, just like Grandpa used to do.

As we sat there, Clark began telling me about his childhood.

"I don't remember my Ma," he began. "She died when I was just two and a half. I guess she had been sick for quite some time. When she got much worse, Pa decided to take her on the train to the hospital in Rochester, Minnesota. She died there. My sisters told me they remembered Pa putting Ma's rocking chair on top of the truck to take along so she had her favorite chair to sit in while in the hospital. She waved goodbye to them as they drove off. That was the last time they saw Ma alive. Pa was able to load it onto the train for the long trip. After Ma and Pa got to Rochester, I don't think she lived long enough to even sit in her rocker. When Pa had to bring Ma back in a casket, he brought the rocker back with him, and it still sits in our living room today.

"We learned when we became adults that Ma was expecting and was seven months along with her eleventh child. She had also lost an infant, a baby girl named Ruth. We always refer to her as Baby Ruth.

"Ma left five children under the age of ten for my father to raise by himself. I had a brother, Paul, who was twenty-one when she died, but he was out on his own. Then my sister, Elva, was nineteen, and Helen was seventeen. They pretty much took over as our mother, caring for us younger kids. My other brother, Kent, was fifteen, then Dorothy was ten, Doris was nine, Martha was seven, Edna was four, and I was two and a half. We were quite a handful for Pa and the older girls."

Clark continued, "I remember wishing I had a mother many times. Once I had a teacher who was so nice and let me sit on her lap. I wished she could be my mother. Then we had an aunt who was married to my mother's brother, Gates Wetzbarger. He died young, about a year before Ma died. He was about thirty-three. It was some kind of accident, I guess. He left eight children behind, the oldest being about ten and the youngest only two months old. I remember Aunt Ethel was so kind and soft and smelled so good when she brought me on her lap. I thought that she and Pa should get married, but I guess with her eight children and our nine, that would make a pretty big household. We got together with them quite often since they didn't live far from us. It was always a happy time when the Wetzbarger cousins came to visit," he said with a smile.

"Well, I guess it's time to get you back to the dorm, Miss Mary Ellen," he said as he took my hand and started walking me back to campus. We took our time and enjoyed each other's company. There was no need to hurry.

That was just one of our many long walks to the ice cream parlor, or sometimes we'd go to a fifteen-cent movie. I wasn't sure about going to movies, as Papa and Mama didn't approve, but Clark loved musicals. He sang in the college choir and played the clarinet in the band, besides playing basketball. He was almost too busy for me to get time with him.

That fall was the sweetest time for me. That Christmas, as we sat in the girl's dorm by the lighted Christmas tree, he leaned over and gave me a soft kiss on my cheek. It was the first time I had ever been kissed by a boy. My heart jumped, and I had this warm feeling in the pit of my stomach. I laughed nervously, but he put me completely at ease by putting his strong arm around my shoulders. We sat like that for a long time. Of course, the dorm mother was right there watching to make sure no hanky-panky took place. Much too soon it was time for him to go. I walked him to the door, and he leaned down and gave me another kiss on the cheek. "Good night, Mary Ellen," he said and then turned and walked away. I stood and watched him as he walked across the campus. He was everything I wanted. So young and handsome, so strong and protective.

My feet barely touched the floor as I went back to my room. I was walking on air. Sharon was waiting to hear about my date. "So, is he your Mr. Right?" she asked as I entered the room.

I sat on my bed, pulled my legs up under me and sighed. "I think so. I don't think I could find anyone as wonderful as Clark for a boyfriend. And guess what? He kissed me two times tonight! Just on the cheek, but it was wonderful. We sat for a long time with his arm around me in front of the Christmas tree talking. I have never been this happy. I can't wait for Mama and Papa to meet him. I just know they will like him as much as I do. I'll tell them all about him when I go home for Christmas next week. It will be hard not seeing Clark for almost a month while we're home. But it will make seeing each other all the more special when we come back."

With all the excitement of the night, I had a hard time getting to sleep. The thoughts of Clark with his arm around me and the two kisses kept playing in my mind. When I said my prayers, I thanked God for giving me such a wonderful Christian man. Only God knew what the future would bring, but I couldn't wait to live it.

Clark Baird about age twelve, circa 1931

THE SAD GOODBYE
1939

I WAS HOME FOR THE summer before my last year in college. It was hard leaving Clark at the train station as we went our separate ways for the summer. I would miss him so much—miss the way he whistled all the time and would break out into song at any moment. He had a wonderful voice, and I loved going to see him sing in the choir at church. He loved to sing to me also, songs like "Don't Sit Under the Apple Tree with Anyone Else but Me" and "Let Me Call You Sweetheart."

He called on my twenty-first birthday. I knew he would. "Hello, sweetheart!" he said. We talked for over an hour. We made plans for when we returned to college in a few weeks. It was hard to say goodbye, but I had to go, as Papa had already headed out to the barn to do the milking.

"Bye-bye, sweetheart, see you soon," Clark said as we hung up. Oh, how I wished I would see him soon. September seemed like such a long way off. My footsteps were heavy as I walked to the barn to help Papa.

One morning, about a week after my birthday, Edith came out of Mama's room and said, "Papa, I can't get Mama to wake up. I have tried calling her name and shaking her, but there is no response. Come see what you think."

We all filed into Mama's room to take a look. She was sleeping, but her breathing was different. "I'm afraid she may have had a stroke," Edith said. "Maybe we should call the doctor and ask him to come take a look at her." I just stood there and stared at Mama. *No, this can't be the end,* I thought to myself.

While Papa went to the phone to call the doctor, I took Mama's hand, and it was limp. I called her name and caressed her cheek with my hand. Her skin was cold and clammy, not the usual soft skin she always had.

When the doctor arrived, he confirmed that she probably had a major stroke. He said that she should be admitted to the hospital so she could be treated and taken care of. He called the ambulance, and in no time they were there, loading Mama carefully into the ambulance.

We followed the ambulance into Canton and when Mama was settled in her room, Dr. Park came to talk to us.

"She has suffered a major stroke, and she may only live days to maybe a week. We will do what we can to keep her comfortable. I think you should go on home, and we will call you if anything changes.

The ride home was a sad one. No one wanted to talk about Mama for fear they would break down. We had gotten a little lunch at the hospital, so when we got home, we went about doing the chores that needed to be done. Edith cleaned up the breakfast dishes, and I went out with Papa to check the cattle. "Papa, are you going to be okay if Mama dies?" I asked timidly.

Papa sat down on the milking stool in the barn and buried his face in his hands and cried. His shoulders shook, and I didn't know what to say, so I just went and stood by his side and put my hand on his shoulder.

Soon he looked up and said, "Nellie has been the light in my world for so many years. I don't know if I can take the darkness that will come when she is gone. I thought I was prepared for the end, but I guess when it really happens, it hits you hard."

We stayed in the comfort of the barn for a long time, talking about Mama and how we will miss her. It still didn't seem real. It was like I was dreaming and would wake up and find Mama up and busy doing the things she used to do every day.

On August 1st, Mama took her last breath with her little family at her side. Papa held her hand a long time after she passed. "She had a full life, even though it was cut short. She had two beautiful girls and got to see them grow into wonderful women. That was all she wanted—to see her girls grow up," he said.

We all said our goodbyes to Mama, then turned and left her room. It still didn't seem real to me. It just hadn't hit me yet that my Mama was gone.

The funeral was two days later. Papa and Edith were holding up pretty well, and I was too until my friend Ethel and her mother came up to me afterwards and said how sorry they were for my loss. Then it hit me—*Mama was gone.*

When I got home, I went straight to my room and cried tears like I have never cried before. I cried myself to sleep and had a dream about Mama. She was young and running in a field of flowers. She stopped and picked a bouquet and gave them to me. She said, "Mary Ellen, you take care of these flowers and remember how much I loved all of you." Then I woke up and looked around, half thinking I would hear Mama calling up the stairs for me to come down for supper, but the house was quiet.

The day Papa took me to the train station to go back to Mitchell, I hugged Edith goodbye and told Papa he could drive to Canton, because I couldn't see for the tears in my eyes. When we pulled out of the yard, I looked back at the old swing swaying in the breeze, and I remembered the hours Mama used to push me in it. The house somehow looked cold and empty. This is the first time I felt like I was leaving as an adult, not as a child, and things seemed different somehow. I learned that summer that you never know how much people mean to you until you lose them.

When the train pulled into the station in Mitchell, there was Clark with Mr. Pearson. I thought my chest would explode with excitement. I waved out the window, and as soon as I alighted from the train, Clark was there and took me into his arms and kissed me, right in front of Mr. Pearson. I didn't care though; I needed his arms around me to comfort me after my mother's passing. He held me for a long time, then arm in arm we walked to Mr. Pearson's car. Mr. Pearson had already put my trunk in the car.

We sat in the back seat and Clark kept his arm around me, as if to say, "I'm not going to let you go again." He finally said, "Mary

Ellen, you don't know how much I have missed you this summer. I almost borrowed a car to come see you. I have all your letters and have read and re-read them, dreaming of the day we'd be together again. I'm so sorry about your mother."

"I missed you too," I said. "I read all your letters many times while sitting under our big tree in the front yard. I still can't believe Mama is gone. It just seems like a dream. The funeral was the worst. Just looking at her in the casket, but I didn't break down until I got home that day. I cried and cried, but then I thought about all the good times we had with her and how she lived such a Godly life. She left that legacy to Edith and me. We made her proud and I plan on continuing to do things that would make her proud."

Soon we were back at the dorm, and I said goodbye to Clark at the door. "See you at supper," he said after he gave me a peck on the cheek.

My last year in college was going to be an exciting one. I would be finishing my bachelor's degree and Clark and I would make so many wonderful memories together.

One night as we sat on the lawn in front of the dorm, Clark turned to me and said, "Mary Ellen, I am in love with you. I've known this for quite some time, but I didn't want to seem too forward."

My heart started to race, and I could feel my face turning red. I knew that I loved him dearly, but I wasn't quite ready to say it. I just said, "I care a lot for you too."

The fall semester flew past, and then in November, I was devastated when Clark told me he was going to transfer to Northern State Teachers College in Aberdeen. He could finish his degree there and planned to stay with his brother Kent to save money.

"No!" I said, "I love you too much to be apart from you." There, I had said it too, and I knew he was the one I wanted to spend the rest of my life with.

"Mary Ellen, I knew my scholarship was going to run out before I finished my degree. I just don't see any other way to do it. It's only one semester. This summer I'll come and visit you and your family," he said with a catch in his voice.

I put my arms around him and gave him a big kiss. "I'll try to be brave, honey. I'll keep busy with my final classes and tests. Can you come to my graduation?" I asked.

"I'll sure try. Maybe my brother will let me use his car. It's going to be hard for me too, but I plan on getting a job and working while I take classes," he said as he took my hand in his. "Let's take a long walk and get some ice cream."

Yes, too soon it would be Christmas vacation and we would be heading in different directions. I just didn't know how I could make it next semester without seeing him every day. But right now, I was walking with him, holding his hand, and talking about our plans for the future. I knew we would be together somehow, but I wasn't sure how everything would work out. I guessed I would leave it in God's hands. He's the one who brought us together in the first place.

THE EMPTY CHAIR

THE DAY MR. PEARSON took me to the train station, Clark was there also, heading home to Frankfort. We sat together in the train station holding hands, saying how much we would miss each other. I was excited to be going home to see my family, but it hurt to say goodbye to Clark, because I knew we would not see each other for quite some time as he was transferring to Northern State. Clark's train was leaving an hour after mine, so he came to spend a little time with me before I left.

Soon my train pulled into the station, and Clark took my hand and walked me to the platform. He put his arms around me and kissed me softly, this time on the lips. That kiss made it even harder to leave him. "Goodbye, Mary Ellen," he said as I pulled away to get on the train.

When I found my seat, I waved my hankie at him and blew kisses to him out the window. He waved back. Even when my train was pulling out, he continued to wave to me from the platform. Then he turned and walked back to the station to wait for his train.

I settled into my seat and thought about the last few months and how my life had changed. When I started college, I just wanted to have fun and not worry too much about grades. Now I was buckling down and getting good grades. My office practice professor was very encouraging to me and felt that I was "good teacher material," as she put it. I had once decided to give up trying to find Mr. Right, but then, out of the blue, there he was standing in front of me. I knew it the moment I first met him. Just one look was all it took.

I couldn't imagine my life without Clark now. Even though we hadn't talked about marriage, it was clear that he loved me, and I loved him dearly. I carried a picture of him that he had given to me. He wrote on the back, 'From a pal to a great gal'. I could hardly wait to show Papa and Edith my new love, Clark.

My mind rested on thoughts of Clark as the train sped closer and closer toward Canton. I thought about the things we'd talked about doing at home during Christmas vacation.

I must have dozed off when suddenly the conductor yelled, "Canton!" I opened my eyes sleepily and looked around. I'm home again. There was Papa standing on the platform waiting for me.

We got my suitcase and headed to the car. The first thing I asked Papa was, "How are you doing without Mama now?"

"We're getting along, but it's hard not to be able to see her and talk to her every day," he said. "Mary Ellen, I have never been so lonely as now. It is a big help that Edith stayed on to keep me company and keep house for me.

"Oh, Papa," I said, trying not to let him hear the tightening of my throat or see the tears on the brink of running down my cheeks. "I'm glad that Edith is staying on with you too. I don't worry so much about you when she's with you."

When we got home and I walked into the kitchen, Edith was there fixing dinner. It smelled wonderful as usual. I half expected to see Mama standing there in her apron making a pie. I almost asked Edith, "Where is Mama?" but I caught myself. Even though she had been bed ridden the last time I saw her, the kitchen seemed empty without her. Everywhere I looked there were touches of Mama, from the pretty homemade curtains with lace in the window to the arrangement of the furniture in the living room. There was her rocking chair sitting in its usual place. On it was the pillow she had made, with black velvet and a pink cross on the front. *Oh, Mama, I thought, how I miss you. I want to tell you all about Clark and have him meet you. I know you would have liked him right away. He reminds me of Papa, the strong silent type.*

After taking my suitcase to my room, I went down to the kitchen where Papa and Edith were having coffee. I couldn't hold my feelings back anymore. I burst into tears and Edith came to my side and hugged me tight. "I know it's hard, Mary Ellen," she said as she rubbed my back. "We've had more time to get used to the fact that she'll never be with us again. Now, dry your tears and let's have some coffee. We want to hear everything about this boy you call Mr. Right."

I was so thankful that I had such a caring and good friend in my sister. We didn't always have that kind of relationship, but now that we were both adults, we were closer than we had ever been before.

Soon Edith got up to get dinner on the table. I could hardly wait to eat one of her meals again. I busied myself with setting the table and helped Edith with the cooking. We decided to eat in the cozy kitchen with the sunlight shining in the big windows. After Papa said the prayer, we dug in. There was a lot of conversation going on, but the empty chair sitting next to Papa was like the empty place in our hearts. The place that Mama always filled.

"Edith," I said after we finished dinner and were doing the dishes together, "I know I could never do what you did for our Mama. Thank you for being such a loving daughter and caring for all her needs. It couldn't have been easy."

"I look at it as my calling," she answered. "I really enjoy taking care of people who aren't able to care for themselves. It was a double blessing to be able to do that for Mama.

Christmas just wasn't the same without Mama, but we had Aunt Mary and Uncle Charlie over for dinner. With Aunt Mary, there is never a lapse in the conversation. She had so many funny stories about her days as a teacher. Now she substituted, which she liked, so she could keep her fingers in the teaching profession.

On New Year's Day I got a big surprise. The phone rang about two o'clock in the afternoon, the familiar two shorts and one long. I ran to get it. "Hello," I said into the receiver.

"Well, hello, is this Miss Mary Ellen Sletten?" I knew as soon as I heard his voice it was Clark.

"Hello, I didn't expect to hear your voice today," I answered.

We talked for almost a half an hour. He even asked to talk to Papa. That made Papa like him even more. It was hard to hang the earpiece up on the hook, but it made my heart soar to hear his voice again. The rest of the day I was on cloud nine thinking about him.

32

GRADUATION DAY

I LIVED FOR THE TIME the mail came each day, hoping for another letter from Clark. He said he was pretty busy with school and was working for a blind man, taking care of him and his house.

"I've learned to cook and clean, a good thing to know when you are batching it," he said in his last letter. I wrote to him daily and told him all about what was happening on campus. Graduation was set for the twentieth of May, and I could hardly wait to see Clark again. He told me he wanted to marry me, but no ring has surfaced.

I already had a teaching job lined up in Canning, South Dakota, a little town close to our state capital of Pierre. I would be home for the summer, and in the fall I would start my new job. I was excited to have a teaching job, and because I had my bachelor's degree, it had a pretty good salary. Clark was going to continue at Northern State for two more years until he would have his bachelor's degree. We talked about getting jobs at the same school and teaching together, but when spring came around, Clark talked more and more about wanting to farm.

"There's just something about being out in nature and working the land, planting, and harvesting the crops. You can't beat that with a stick," he said in his last letter. Then he drew a smiley face. "Your dad mentioned to me that if I wanted to take over his farm, he would be honored. He said he didn't know how much longer he was going to farm, and he wants to get into a pastor's position before he gets too old."

I thought about that all day after I got his letter. I loved the farm, of course, but I wanted to teach school. It just wouldn't be practical for me to have a teaching position in town and live on the farm. I dreamed about how it would be to work side by side with Clark. It seemed romantic to be together working and making the farm our own. Well, I would have to think about it. After all, he hadn't even given me a ring yet.

On graduation day I waited outside the girl's dorm for Clark to arrive. Pretty soon a car drove up and honked, and I saw it was Clark. I ran to the car and jumped in. He drew me to him and we kissed. "Missy, I have missed you so much," he said.

I loved it when he called me Missy, and I hoped that he had a graduation gift for me that would go on the third finger of my left hand. But right now, I was about to graduate from college. We were only going from the girl's dorm to the auditorium, which we could have walked, but he wanted to drive me. This was something new for us as he didn't have a car himself, and we had always walked everywhere before. He had borrowed his brother Kent's car for the trip to Mitchell.

The graduation ceremony was on Saturday, and Clark stayed at the Pearson's until Sunday so we could have more time together.

We did the usual things, like going to get ice cream and having long talks about what the future holds.

"Mary Ellen, I was so proud of you when you walked across the stage to get your diploma," he said. "I don't know if a college diploma is for me. I have been thinking that I may not return to school in the fall. I may take your dad up on helping him with the farm. That seems like a great opportunity for me. I'm not so sure I am cut out to be a teacher. Farming is just in my blood."

"Just remember that I have signed a contract to teach in Canning for one year, so you'll have to be satisfied with talking to Papa and Edith," I said. "I plan to come home on the train for Christmas vacation, but that will be the only time I'll be home. I have to pay back my loan from the Methodist Church. I guess it wouldn't be any different if you were in Aberdeen or Canton. We still wouldn't see each other for six months."

"That seems like a long time," Clark said as he took my hand. "I guess we'll have to keep writing letters back and forth for a while."

My heart jumped when he took hold of my hand, and I thought this was the moment. *Now he is going to pull out his graduation gift and put it on my finger.* But no, he walked me to the car saying he had to get back to Aberdeen before it got dark. He kissed me as he dropped me off at the dorm. "See you soon, Mary Ellen, remember that I love you." Then he was gone.

My heart was heavy as I walked to my dorm room. I had packing to do, because tomorrow I would be taking the train back home, without a ring. I just couldn't figure it out. He said he loves me, and I love him terribly. We talked about marriage, but still no commitment. Oh, men! They could be so wishy-washy at times. Why, I think he was more excited about farming with my dad than being married to me.

My roommate came through the door just then and saw that I was teary. "What's the matter? Did you and Clark have a fight?"

"No, he was so very sweet, as he always is. It's just that I had hoped I would get a ring from him for graduation, but all he could talk about was farming," I said.

"Well, you know that men can have a hard time making a commitment, but I know he is committed to you and you alone," she said. "You don't have to worry about that. Things will work out, you'll see. How about we walk down to the ice cream parlor and have a double dip. That will make you feel better. This is our last day together. I will sure miss you and all our heart-to-heart talks. I wish you could come to my wedding this summer, but I know it's too hard to make the trip and it would cost too much. Just wait, I predict that you will be getting married next summer, you wait and see," she said.

Next summer seemed like a lifetime away. A lot could happen in a year. I wondered how my first year teaching would go. I felt confident in my ability, as I had done some student teaching this year. But I wondered how I could keep my mind on my work without knowing where my relationship with Clark was going.

"Time will tell," Papa told me when I arrived home for the summer. We had been talking about the possibility of having Clark come stay here and help with the farming. "I would feel better for sure if you had a ring on your finger, but I believe he is sincere and will do that in his own time."

"I guess you're right, Papa," I said. "I will just have to learn to be more patient."

It was great to be back home. My friend Ethel was also home for the summer, and we had a great time talking about our high school years and confiding in each other about our college life. We had been writing to each other, so she knew all about Clark.

My birthday was drawing near, only three weeks away. I secretly hoped that Clark would come here for my birthday and surprise me with a ring. I would feel so much better if I had a ring when I moved to Canning to teach. It would say, *I'm taken,* but nothing in his letters even hinted that he had our engagement in mind.

I was busy helping Edith with the garden and Papa with the milking. We had many good talks as we worked, and Edith told me she was looking for a job where she could live in the home and do housework and help take care of the owner. She really wanted to get out on her own and earn her way. She was waiting to see what happened with Clark and me.

"If you two get married and live here, I will feel like a fifth wheel," she said. "That's why I'm looking for a job. I'm pretty certain by next summer you'll be married," she said one night as we finished up the dishes.

Everyone seemed so certain that Clark and I would get married, except me. Why was I so worried about it? Clark loves me and I love him; the ring will come soon enough. I had dreamed about that event for so long, and I was beginning to think that it may never happen. "Lord, help me to be patient and to trust that you will allow what is best for Clark and me," I prayed that night. Tomorrow was July fourth and I wished Clark could be there to celebrate with me, but I had no word that he was even thinking about coming. He had talked about coming for my birthday, so I held on to that, hoping he would come with a ring.

33

Fourth of July Surprise

The next day was the Fourth of July. I always looked forward to it, as we usually went to Beresford to watch the fireworks. Edith and I had made up a nice lunch to take with us, and the car was all gassed up and washed, ready for the trip.

I was being lazy and didn't want to get out of bed that morning. Edith suddenly appeared in the doorway to my room and said, "You have a visitor, Mary Ellen."

She had a little gleam in her eye, and I couldn't figure out who it would be at this time in the morning. I hurriedly dressed, and when I came down the stairs, who do you think was standing there?

"Clark!" I exclaimed. "What in the world are you doing here? You didn't tell me you were coming, or I would have been more presentable."

He walked over to me and gave me a big hug and kiss. I was a little embarrassed as Edith and Papa were standing there in the dining room. "I just couldn't wait until later in July to see my girl," Clark said as he continued to hold me in his arms. "Now, this guy is mighty hungry, how about some breakfast?"

"I'll make you some eggs and pancakes. Would that be okay?" I asked as I led him into the kitchen and sat him down at the table. Instantly, everything seemed right. Clark was here, and I was going to make him breakfast. Just how I hoped things would be for the rest of our lives. I somehow didn't care that I didn't have a ring on my finger. I was just so happy that he came to see me. I couldn't have asked for anything else.

We talked as I bustled around mixing the pancakes and frying the eggs. Out of the blue, I saw Clark get up off the chair and come stand next to me. Then he knelt on one knee and pulled out a small blue case from his pocket. When he opened it, I saw a beautiful diamond ring, and he said, "Mary Ellen, will you marry me?"

Tears came to my eyes as he took the ring and put it on my finger. "Yes!" I said. Then we kissed again, and I almost let the eggs burn. If it weren't for Edith watching, they might have gone up in smoke.

It was quite the Fourth of July—one I will never forget, and I will hold the memory of that day forever. When we got home from Beresford, Clark and I took a long walk out into the pasture. The grass was green and waving in the breeze, and the cows stood like statues watching us as we walked past, as if to say, "Who do you think you are, walking in our pasture?" We didn't pay any attention; we only had eyes for each other. We had a lot to discuss now. When the wedding would be, if Clark would go back to Northern State, where would we live after our wedding.

"We don't have to figure everything out tonight," Clark said as we walked back to the house. "I plan on staying here a week so we can get things worked out. I've been writing to your dad, and he offered for me to stay here with him come fall. I'll help him with the harvest, and when you finish your year teaching, we can be married."

I could hardly believe everything was happening, just as I had hoped. During that week, we set our wedding date for the next summer, June 1, 1941, just as soon as I was finished teaching. I did think about the fact that I probably wouldn't teach after I got married, because schools frowned upon married women teachers. That was okay with me. I was so happy I thought I would burst. I was going to be Mrs. Clark Baird in one year.

We all went to church together that Sunday, and I introduced Clark and showed off my new ring. Ethel and some of my friends from high school were there. She squealed with delight when I showed her my ring. "Ethel, if you're home next summer, would you be my maid of honor?" I asked. Ethel replied, "If I am home, I would be honored to stand up for you."

Soon it was time for Clark to head back home. He was helping his dad around the farm this summer. He took me in his arms and kissed me before he got into the car and drove down the driveway. I ran around the house to wave at him as he pulled out onto the road, and then I ran to the end of the driveway and waved until his car disappeared over the rise. I slowly walked back to the house as I gazed at the beautiful ring on my finger.

My birthday that year was uneventful. I remembered how I had hoped Clark would surprise me with a ring for my birthday. He really did surprise me, but I never thought it would've been on the Fourth of July.

I spent the rest of the summer making some new dresses to wear for teaching and packing things I would need for the year. I would be boarding with a Mr. and Mrs. Crooker in Canning. Clark was going to come and take me to my new school at the beginning of September, and I would start my teaching career. It was going to be a long six months without seeing Clark before Christmas, but I felt good knowing he was going to be staying with Papa and helping him with the harvest and milking.

Clark arrived at the farm a few days before I was to leave. He brought all his clothes and moved them in with Papa. He didn't think it would be proper to take a room upstairs with Edith sleeping up there. He and Papa agreed to share a bed in the downstairs bedroom. I could only imagine two men over six feet tall trying to stay out of each other's space.

The day we left for Canning, Papa and Edith stood out on the driveway saying goodbye. Clark and I didn't have to say goodbye yet. We had a nice long drive to Canning, so we got started early. We had a lunch packed in the back with all my clothes and other things. It was a little tight, but Clark didn't say a word, just got the car loaded. He had come in on the train, so Papa was letting us use his car for the trip. We waved as we drove out the driveway, then I slid over and sat close to Clark and he put his arm around me. I felt warm all over. It felt so right.

Clark teased me about what we would find in Canning. "I bet there will be a town pump for water and outhouses for the school," he said. "You will probably have the oldest, rustiest typewriters around, and most of the kids will come to school barefoot."

I hit him on the shoulder and said, "Oh, stop teasing me, I'm nervous enough without worrying about those things." We laughed and enjoyed the trip.

We stopped at Clark's home outside of Frankfort to meet his dad. I was a little afraid of meeting him. Clark told me about his home. "It's nothing to look at. I don't think it has ever seen a paint brush as long as I can remember, but it is home to me."

Clark had told his dad all about me and said he thought he'd like me because I was so kind and gentle, just like he thought his mother had been. We shared our packed lunch with Dad Baird, and I liked him right away. He was very quiet, not at all like my Papa, but he was very kind also. He seemed to be pleased with our wedding plans and that Clark was going to stay with my Papa and help him this fall and next spring. I was a little surprised when I first saw him, as he was very short. I expected him to be tall like Clark, but he was a small, little man, with a big heart.

When I saw Clark's childhood home, I couldn't help but think what a contrast it was to the home where I grew up. We had a big, white square house with four bedrooms upstairs and one downstairs, a dining room, and a large living room and kitchen. So much space for only four people. Clark's dad's house was quite small with only two bedrooms upstairs and one downstairs. It really did look quite rough without any paint on it. I couldn't imagine a family with nine children living there. It definitely looked lived in. No pretty curtains in the windows or rugs on the floor.

It made me feel close to Clark as he showed me around their farm. I could imagine him as a little boy running and playing in that yard with his siblings. I felt a little jealous thinking about him having all those siblings to play with while I had to play by myself most of the time.

After lunch we were on our way again. We arrived at Canning to find just what Clark had predicted—a town pump and outhouses. He gave me a look like, "I told you so." Clark helped unload my things into the room where I would be staying. It was small, but very private. I did have to share a bathroom, but there was also an outhouse. Mr. and Mrs. Crooker were very nice and welcomed me to their home.

Clark and I drove past the schoolhouse just to have a look at it and then back to Crookers' house where we had to say goodbye. "See you in December," Clark said. "I will be counting the days. It's going to be a long drive back to your farm without you by my side to talk to."

We had kissed goodbye at the schoolhouse because we didn't want to be too sappy in front of the Crookers'. I just waved as he drove down the street. My heart ached, and I didn't know how I was going to stand it until Christmas. I went slowly back into the house. Mrs. Crooker had a nice meal for me that night, and I went to bed, thinking about Clark and wondering if he was back at the farm. I had a hard time getting to sleep that night as I was excited about my first day of teaching tomorrow. I thanked God that night, for giving me Clark and this teaching job, and for the Crookers' home where I would spend the next year. "Help me to be a good teacher and make the year fly by fast," I said as I ended my prayer.

MISS SLETTEN

I DIDN'T SLEEP WELL THAT night for thinking about Clark and our planned wedding in June. And even though the Crookers were very nice people, I was in a strange new place which added to my sleeplessness. This was going to be a long year. I was excited to get started in my teaching career here in Canning, but I was also very nervous. Would I be able to handle the kids, some only a few years younger than me? The principal said I would have about ten students in my class, a manageable size, but I couldn't help having butterflies in my stomach as I walked to the schoolhouse the next morning.

I stopped at the principal's office, and he gave me the schedule for my classes. I would be teaching Typing I and II, supervising a study hall, advising the school paper, and taking turns with playground duty. He also asked if I would be willing to coach the girls' softball team in the spring. This took me by surprise, as I was not exactly known for excelling in sports. My mind took me back to old Pleasant Ridge and the trauma I endured, always being the last one chosen for a team. I "couldn't hit the broad side of a barn," Russell Hunt used to say. But I did know all about the game from sitting on the sidelines and watching most of the time.

Actually, I did make a home run once in eight years of grade school. I was as shocked as anyone that day. Russell was pitching, and when the ball came to me, I swung with my eyes shut like I usually did. I felt the ball make contact with the bat and opened my eyes to see it had gone right between the pitcher and third base. I knew I was a fast runner, so I took off like a shot for first base. Russell got the ball when I was about halfway there and threw it with all his might. It went over the head of the first baseman, so I kept running. The same happened on second base, so I rounded third, thinking I just might be able to get home. The catcher missed catching the ball, which should have gotten me out. I ran across home plate as if I was a seasoned athlete. Everyone shouted and cheered for me. I felt like I was six feet tall.

I accepted the girls' softball coach position. *Clark won't believe it when I tell him,* I thought, *and neither will Papa and Edith.*

I found my classroom and started putting up the bulletin board decorations that Edith and I made over the summer. My room was small, but it looked homey now that I had bright things posted on the bulletin board. I tried remembering what I learned when I practice-taught in Mitchell last year. It was a good experience and gave me confidence that I could teach.

Soon the bell rang, and students started to file into the classroom. The first class I had was Freshmen Typing I. They all looked so young, and I wondered if they had even seen a typewriter before. So, my first day of teaching started.

By the end of the day, I was exhausted and wasn't so sure I was cut out for teaching. I didn't have the same spring in my step on my way home as I had that morning.

The Crookers had some chores for me to do after school, and one was feeding the chickens and gathering the eggs. I didn't mind, as it was a job I had done since I was small. I loved hearing their clucking as the chickens talked back and forth to each other. I imagined them saying, *Well, good morning, Mrs. Redhen, how are you on this fine day? Or, I told you to leave my food alone,* as one chicken chased another away from the food. I also helped Mrs. Crooker with the cooking and baking. I showed her many recipes that I had learned from Mrs. Pearson, one being a simple salad.

"You start with a single lettuce leaf on the plate, then add a banana sliced in half lengthwise, then peanut butter and a dollop of mayonnaise on top." Mr. Crooker loved the results.

Most of the children I had in class were very respectful and truly loved learning, but some were not so inclined. One was a senior boy who played football and was only learning to type because it was required. He stood head and shoulders over me and barely fit into the desk. He was a little intimidating, but I had learned at an early age how to handle myself. I did feel a little sorry for him, with his large hands trying to hit each key with accuracy. I tried to encourage him, and he soon warmed up to me and became one of my best students. He couldn't type very fast, but he really improved over time.

One day in late November I received a letter from Clark. He usually wrote to me at least a couple times a week. They were never very long as he was not one to talk a lot, but I loved hearing what he was doing and, of course, hearing that he loved me. When I finally got some time alone in my room that night, I opened the letter and read it three or four times.

Dear Mary Ellen (coach),

I couldn't help teasing you a little about being a coach. I'm sure you have all those girls whipped into shape and they will have a winning season next spring.

I miss you so much and every day I count the days until you'll come home for Christmas vacation. It will be wonderful to see you and have you in my arms again. Your Papa and I have made a little change to my sleeping arrangement around here. We both were not getting much sleep trying to stay out of the other's way all night. I have taken a cot in the small bedroom, the one on the north side of the living room. Your Papa told me that it was the room where you were born and told me the story about that day. I know that God had you in mind for me when he brought you into the world. Just think, if my Ma would have died before I was born and your Mama died before you were born, we would not be here. Oh, how sad that would have been. I thank my Ma every day that she gave me life.

Soon this house will be our home together, and just think of all the adventures we will have as husband and wife. Maybe a few little feet will someday be pitter-pattering around here.

I love you so much and am counting the days until you get home.

Your soon-to-be husband, Clark

I read and re-read that letter so many times I almost wore the paper out folding and unfolding it. I had something I could tease him about too—his first name was really Henry and Clark was his middle name, but he wanted to be called Clark. He would sign his name H. Clark Baird. When I really wanted to tease him, I would say, "Oh, Henry, I just love your black hair," or "Henry, would you mind walking me to the ice cream parlor?"

The thought of us being husband and wife made my heart pound. *I'm going to be Mrs. Clark Baird.* I practiced writing it over and over just to see it on paper. *Mrs. Clark Baird, Mrs. H. Clark Baird, Mrs. Mary Ellen Baird.* I never got tired of seeing it written. The time seemed to drag as I waited for Christmas vacation, but finally the day came, and I boarded the train that would take me home to Clark.

The train usually looked like it was speeding along the track, but it seemed to be chugging at five miles an hour that day. It had to stop at every town along the way. I thought, *Just skip this town, no one is getting on anyway.* But they stopped and waited and then we were on our way again. I dozed some and was awakened by the conductor saying, "Next stop, Canton." I knew Clark was going to be meeting me at the station, so I checked my lipstick and brushed through my hair. I wanted to look the best I could, even after riding the train all day.

As we pulled into the little station, I looked around for Clark. There he was, standing on the platform with his topcoat and his fedora on. He looked like a movie star! How could it be that I was going to be his wife? As I stepped off the train, he rushed to my side and took me in his arms and kissed me. He had never kissed me like that before, but I liked it. I would have a lifetime of kisses from Clark. We got my suitcase and were soon heading to the farm. We had so much to talk about that it seemed like the trip home only took five minutes. Papa and Edith were happy to see me and welcomed me with big hugs. I was a little bit jealous of Edith, as she got to spend every day with Clark, and she washed his clothes and ironed his shirts for him, but I could tell, Clark only had eyes for me.

When Papa and Clark went out to do the milking, Edith and I busied ourselves getting supper ready for them when they came in from the barn. It was good to talk to my sister and tell her everything about my teaching job. "I am sorry that teaching didn't work out for you, Edith. I just love it and hope to be able to teach many more years, at least before Clark and I have our family," I said, turning red. I had never talked to Edith about such things.

"I know all about what happens after people get married," Edith replied. "It is a natural thing, and the children you and Clark will have will all be beautiful. I don't know if I will ever find someone for me, but I will spoil your children as if they were mine."

What a wonderful time we had that Christmas. We all went to church together, and Clark gave me a beautiful necklace with a locket. He had put a picture of us in it. I gave him some new leather gloves so he didn't have to wear those old raggedy ones with his coat and hat for church. We finished making all the plans for our wedding, to be held on the first of June next year. It was finally seeming real, and nothing could stop it now. It would be a small wedding with only a few friends and family. Clark hoped his dad would come, but he didn't hold out hope, as his dad hadn't been off the farm for years. He was still farming, what little there was to farm after the drought, and his nephew, Stanley, was helping him also.

The night before I was to return to Canning, we took a long walk out in the brisk night air, with the stars sparkling like diamonds and the moon shining over the snow-covered landscape. He had his arm around me and pulled me close to him to keep me warm. I would remember that night forever. I had never been so happy and in love than at that very moment, but something was hanging over us, something that threatened to change all our plans.

"I'm worried," I said, "with all this talk about war, there could be another world war. What if you have to go and fight? What if you didn't make it back home? We may never be able to get married or have a family. I just couldn't stand it if that happened."

Clark took me into his arms and held me for a long time. "Mary Ellen, nothing will stop our love. We just have to trust that God won't allow anything that wouldn't be for the best," Clark said. "I can't say that I would never fight if there were a war. I feel strongly about defending our country and its freedoms, but let's cross that bridge when and if we get there. Right now, we are together and in love and come June first, nothing will stop me from marrying you, Mary Ellen Sletten," he said before giving me a sweet kiss. "Now we better get back inside and warm up. We've had such a wonderful time together, but just you wait until June first!"

Clark took me to the station the next day, and we had a long goodbye on the platform before I boarded the train. As the train pulled out of the station, I waved at Clark, and he waved back at me. I already missed him so much. How would I ever get through these next six months?

WEDDING BELLS

IT WAS HARD TO be back in Canning after Christmas vacation, but I was in the swing of teaching and that kept my mind off missing Clark so much. *It wouldn't be long now,* I kept telling myself as I marked off the days on the calendar. Clark would be back to get me on the fifteenth of May. I would miss the kids in my classes and the other teachers who were so encouraging to me. My first year of teaching would come to a close, but a new chapter of my life would be starting. June first, Clark and I would be married and start our life together on the farm.

The months passed quickly and soon it was April first, and I started coaching the girls' softball team, the Canning Canaries. They were a great group of girls. They really knew how to play soft-ball, therefore they needed very little coaching from me. It was fun watching them play. How they could hit! I became very attached to them in the short time that I coached them. I was good at cheering them on and basking in their reflected glory. We played fifteen games that season and won fourteen of them. I was so proud of their accomplishments. Some nights I came home hoarse from cheering.

We had been hearing on the radio news about the war going on in other parts of the world for some time. The United States was not involved in the war, and I was thankful for that, but they had started what they called "compulsory military training," which meant they were calling men to be trained. Many of my male students talked about it a lot, and some had already signed up and would be going right after graduation. I worried about Clark being called up but prayed that he wouldn't. I remember how Grandpa Sletten would shed tears at the grave of his youngest son, Anthony, who died in the Great War. I didn't think I could make it through something like that.

The twenty-eighth of April started like most other days in Canning High School. About noon I was called into the principal's office. There stood Clark! I could hardly believe he was really there. "Did you get your dates mixed up?" I asked. "You were supposed to come get me May fifteenth."

Looking a little sheepish, he asked if we could talk in private. *What could be wrong? Did something happen to Papa?* I started to panic, but Clark took my hand, and we went out to the picnic table in back of the school.

"I think we should get married tomorrow," he said with a look of love in his eyes. "Your dad said we should not wait until June, because he fears that I will be called up. He is sure the U.S. will be entering the war sooner than later. I know this is very sudden, but I really think your dad is right, and I trust his judgment."

"But we already have a wedding date set for June first," I protested. "I have made a lot of plans for the biggest day of my life. Where can we get married on this short notice? Plus, I need to get some time off from school, which might not be easy." I had a few tears by this time.

Clark gave me his hanky with which I wiped away the tears. "I have already talked to your principal about you taking half a day off tomorrow and he has agreed. So, everything is set. We can drive to Pierre tomorrow after you get off at noon and we can be married by five," Clark said. Then he took me in his arms, and I knew I had to agree. It felt like my heart was beating a hundred miles an hour.

"Usually, schools don't allow married women to teach, but I know that is changing," I said.

"Your principal doesn't have a problem with you finishing out this year being married. What do you say, Mary Ellen?" he asked hopefully.

"I say yes! Let's do it," I said. "I can't believe I will come back to school on Monday as Mrs. Baird. What will the kids say?" I couldn't help thinking about them and what they would say. They knew I was planning on getting married in June, but this would be the talk of the school.

That night I could hardly sleep for the excitement. Clark stayed with the Crookers and slept on the couch. We talked about having him take most of my things back home with him. Then when he came back on May fifteenth, I wouldn't have much to move out.

The next day Clark drove me to school, then took the car to get gas and ready it for our short trip to Pierre. Teaching that morning was very hard for me. I told all my students that I was getting married that afternoon, and they were very happy for me. They had all kinds of questions and well-wishes.

Finally, the noon bell rang and as the students filed out of class, they all wished me many happy years together. Clark was outside waiting in the car for our trip to Pierre. I wore my best dress to school that day, so I was ready when Clark pulled up. Mr. and Mrs. Crooker were going along to stand up for us. When I got in the car, Clark handed me a box. I opened it to find a beautiful corsage inside.

"Oh, Clark, you have thought of everything." With shaking hands, he pinned it onto my dress, then gave me a kiss. There were kids looking on and they all cheered as we drove off.

"All we need now," Clark said, "is some old shoes and cans tied to the bumper. Maybe some limburger cheese on the engine."

"So, do you know where the courthouse is in Pierre?" I asked.

"I sure do," Clark replied. But when we got to Pierre, we had to drive around a little to locate it, but we soon found it and were standing in front of the justice of the peace.

The next thing I knew, we were saying our vows and the justice of the peace pronounced us man and wife. Clark kissed me, the first kiss of our married life, and we were walking on air as we left the courthouse as a married couple with our marriage certificate in hand. We stopped to get something to eat before we drove back to Canning. I could hardly eat for the excitement of the day. Clark had slept on the sofa at the Crookers' last night; however, tonight he would be staying in my small room.

When we got back to the Crookers', we called my Papa and his dad to let them know the good news. Papa and Edith were very excited and couldn't wait for us to get home. About eight that night, we told the Crookers goodnight and went to my room. Clark and I were a little shy about being so close to the Crookers, and I knew the walls were paper thin. We talked for a long time, just holding each other. Clark was very understanding, but finally he said, "This is our wedding night. I think they understand that."

"I love you, Clark," I said as I held him tight. "This is our wedding night, the day I have waited so long for." It was a sweet first night as a married couple, and the Crookers did understand.

The next day at school, I got a lot of teasing from the kids, and the teachers all wished us well in our marriage. Some of the boys in my class came to me after school and asked sheepishly, with their feet shuffling, if they could give us a shivaree. They had secured a two-wheeled cart to pull us around town in. "Sure," I said, "that will be fun, and I think Clark would like that too."

That night, the kids arrived at the Crookers' at eight and we were loaded into the cart. They started out at a slow pace as we rounded the school building and down one street and up another. Then things seemed to get a little out of hand. They decided to take us out on a country road that was filled with ruts and large clods of dirt. They started going faster and faster until I thought we would be thrown out and killed. Clark and I kept yelling, "Stop! Please Stop!" But they didn't seem to hear us. We were both clinging to each other, and I was hiding my face in Clark's shirt, praying they would soon stop. It seemed like hours, but it was only about ten minutes, until they slowed down and took us back to the Crookers'. We were never so happy to be back on our two feet. The boys yelled, "Goodbye, Mr. and Mrs. Baird! You sure were good sports." Clark thought I should report the incident to the principal, but I didn't feel like making a big scene in my last two weeks of school. We were none the worse for wear, except for a few bruises, which would fade.

The next day Clark and I worked at getting my things packed up and loaded in the car. Clark would be leaving early in the morning to go back to the farm. In two weeks, he would be back to take me home. *Two weeks,* I thought. *But now I don't have to wait to be married, because we already are.* It would be a long two weeks, but I knew I would be busy. Sunday morning, I waved as Clark pulled onto the street and headed back south to our farm. I fingered my wedding ring as I watched him disappear. "Drive safe!" I yelled after him. He raised his arm and waved, saying he heard me.

After our last softball game a few days later, I brought a home-made chocolate cream cake for us to share. They all raved about it, and we ate the whole thing. They brought me a gift they all had pitched in to buy, a beautiful scarf to wear with my blue coat. A few tears were shed when we all went our separate ways that night.

A week before school let out, the Crookers and I were at a PTA meeting when someone came running in and announced that the Crookers' house was burning. We all rushed back to their house. Mr. Crooker was able to get to my room and grab what clothes he could from the closet and dresser. The house burned to the ground, and later we found that a brooder stove they kept in a little room off the living room to keep the baby chicks warm had caught fire. The only thing they couldn't save was my mother's gold watch which she wore when she taught school. I felt really bad about that, as it was meant to belong to Edith.

That night I went with the Crookers, their two high school girls, and their first-grade boy, to stay at the depot in town. I was thankful that I only had to spend one week there but felt sorry for the

Crookers, as they were poor enough without losing their home. It was quite the experience.

I called Clark using the depot's phone and told him about the fire. "It was terrible," I said through tears. "I wish you were here. I'm thankful you took most of my belongings and that Mr. Crooker was able to save the rest of my clothes."

The community rallied around them in the next few weeks. After I left, I learned that someone had offered a home to them, and the community replaced their furniture and household needs. I only lived there one year, but I realized how important it is to have a community around you to lend a hand if needed.

The fifteenth of May was here before I knew it, and Clark pulled up to the train depot about noon. I ran out to greet him and threw my arms around his neck and gave him a big kiss. "Well, hello, Mrs. Baird," he said with a smile, "are you ready to go home with me now?"

"I've been ready for a long time," I replied as we walked hand in hand. "I'll be glad to sleep someplace where my bed doesn't skitter across the floor when the train goes by." It didn't take long to load my things, and I was so happy that we had decided to send most of my things with Clark in April. After waving goodbye to the Crookers, we started out on our way home. We were going to stop at Clark's dad's place again, and all his sisters and brothers and their families were going to be there to meet me. I was excited to meet all the other siblings that Clark had told me so much about.

As we drove down the highway, I sat next to Clark with his arm around me. How could I be any happier than right now? As he started to whistle the song "I Only Have Eyes for You," I said a silent prayer and thanked God for giving me this wonderful man.

Mary Ellen and Clark Baird's wedding picture
April 29, 1941

Acknowledgments

To my mother, Mary Ellen Sletten Baird, who worked tirelessly to care for her family. Some of the stories in this book are gleaned from stories she told us and wrote about. She was always caring, always encouraging and always showing us what it was like to live a life with dedication to one person, my dad Clark Baird, for sixty-six years. I miss you both every day.

I also want to thank my sisters Ruth Baird Pollard and Dorothy Baird Bos, for their many hours of editing my first draft, and all the encouragement they continually give me.

The cover photo of the little girl was taken by Amy Willson Mayer, of her daughter, Olivia Mayer, who is my granddaughter and a great-granddaughter of Mary Ellen.

About the Author

MARY BAIRD MAYER grew up with five sisters and two brothers on the farm that her grandfather bought in 1917, in the house where her mother was born. Lucky enough to attend country school for seven years before moving to Beresford, South Dakota, she enjoyed her childhood on the same Dakota prairie as her great-grandmother, Isabelle. After high school, she married her husband, Allen, and had four children. Upon earning an Associate Degree in her late twenties, nursing became her profession for thirty-five years. In retirement, she and Allen are blessed with twelve grandchildren and one great-granddaughter. On any given day, you'll find her busy writing, doing craft projects, attending church-related activities, working on Ancestry.com and making music with her accordion group.

ISABELLE: Dakota Pioneer Wife and Mother is an enchanted journey in creative nonfiction narrated from the perspective of the author's great-grandmother. When Ingeborg (Isabelle) Dahl was born in Arvika, Värmland County, Sweden, in 1851 and her parents softly held her for the first time, they could not have fathomed the joys and hardships awaiting their tiny daughter in a foreign land. Isabelle would grow up to be resilient beyond their wildest imaginings.

Available in bookstores online worldwide.